Editor-in-Chief/co-Publisher:	Michael G. Reccia.
Specials Editor:	Andy Pearson.
Art Editor/co-Publisher:	David Openshaw.
Contributors:	Olivier Cabourdin, Jean-Marc Deschamps, Robert S. LePine, Gordon Moriguchi, Lori Miller, Todd Morton, Dave Pearson, Chris Potter, John Reason, Chris Rogerson, David Sisson, Theo P. Stefanski, Steve Walker, James Winch.

Very special thanks to *Gordon Moriguchi* and *Todd Morton* for their invaluable help in compiling this title.

web:
www.scififantasymodeller.co.uk

editorial email:
info@scififantasymodeller.co.uk

Published by Happy Medium Press.

Copyright ©2016
ISBN-13: 978-0-9930320-9-7

Sci-High Models' Swift: *build by Olivier Cabourdin.*

EDITORIAL

Fact, they say, is stranger than fiction.

...Not in all cases, it isn't. Take the actual year 1999 compared to its fictional, small screen counterpart created by Gerry and Sylvia Anderson. Now history, the 'real' 1999 unfolded as a strangely familiar blend of man's inhumanity to man and natural disaster, ending with a fear and loathing of the much anticipated but never manifested Y2K bug. In contrast, the Andersons' fictitious 1999 (created from the flared-trousered, brown and orange wallpapered viewpoint of 1974) envisioned such other-worldly strangeness as a Moon blown out of orbit, *Gwent*, *Piri*, the *SS Daria*, a journey through a Black Sun, a gigantic *Space Brain*, a man haunted by his own spirit, and much more.

So polished, unique and distinct were the images and situations created for **Space:1999** that they are remembered and re-watched with extreme fondness to this very day – welcome distractions from the harshness of real life, constructs of the imagination that model makers have for decades sought to recreate in miniature and in the most exacting detail on hobby workbenches across the world.

You hold in your hands a celebration of all aspects of **Space:1999** modelling, from actual studio miniatures, props and costumes from the series to accurate recreations of craft, vehicles and hardware. So, no matter what the actual year is serving up as you read this (doubtless more of the same – unless we've actually begun to learn better at long last) here's an opportunity to travel back to a retro future so compelling we never tire of recreating and revisiting it, courtesy of the modellers whose considerable talents we are proud and delighted to be able to showcase in these pages.

Enjoy.

Michael G. Reccia
Editor-in-Chief (Happy Medium Press)

CONTENTS

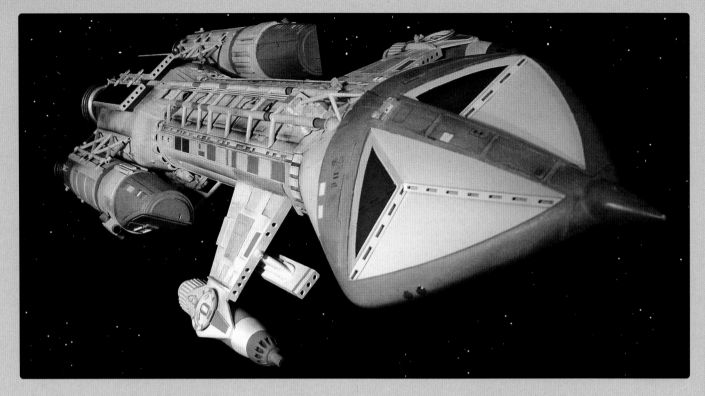

Hawks!
...They're Mark Nine Hawks!

David Sisson builds the classic guest craft from *War Games*

The *Mark IX Hawk* made its one and only appearance in the **Space: 1999** first season episode *War Games*, where a formation of three managed to destroy quite a few *Eagles* and much of *Moonbase Alpha* before our hero, *Commander Koenig*, realised that it was all just a dream!

In these pre-**Star Wars** days this episode was a special effects extravaganza that certainly made an impact on myself and many other people, both young and old. This wasn't lost on the marketing men who brought out a model kit of the *Hawk* as a companion piece to the popular *Eagle Transporter*. As a result this craft is probably the most easily remembered 'guest' model in the series, even though **Space: 1999** featured one of the highest model spaceship counts in television sci-fi history.

While I tend to spend most of my model making time producing replicas of the many principle vehicles from all of the Gerry Anderson television shows I do occasionally tackle a guest craft. Over the years I have had more than a few goes at building the *Hawk* and I am

currently working on my fourth studio-sized replica. The first attempt was back in the late 1980s and at the time I thought that the finished result was a reasonably good model, but sadly it really wasn't because I had fallen into the trap of thinking that the model was just made of 'a few' *Airfix* kits and a custom nosecone/cabin. But no... it is, in fact, made from a lot more model kits than you think and has three times more detail than I first realised!

After that failure I wasn't too keen to have another go because this model isn't actually one of my favourite vehicles, and at the end of the day the original studio model did still exist and was in the hands of a good friend of mine. Because of this I had seen and handled the model a great many times over the years, and had become very used to seeing it around to the point that it seemed rather pointless making a copy. However, this all changed when my friend decided to sell the model to an overseas buyer, and then thrust the *Hawk* into my hands with the request that I build him a copy before it left the

country forever (although saying that it has since come back!).

With the *Hawk* sitting in my workshop it seemed like a good idea to build myself one too, and so the pictures accompanying this article are from those two builds and the current half-completed one.

The *Hawk* was designed by **Space: 1999** Special Effects Supervisor Brian Johnson and then the task of making it was passed to model maker Martin Bower, who not only had to build one high quality 31" hero model but a half scale and 5-inch version as well. In order to build the highly detailed models in such a short time frame Martin resorted to kit-bashing, and as a result a great deal of the *Hawk* is made up of plastic parts taken from readily available model kits.

So the first task for anyone wanting to scratchbuild a *Hawk* is to try and identify as many kit parts as possible, and then try to find all of them. Luckily there are forums on the Internet to help you these days, and you will usually find someone building a *Hawk* and asking for or providing the information you require. So if you are interested in this then you probably know most of them already, but here's my list:

Airfix Harrier – 1:24 scale
Airfix Saturn V rocket – 1:144 scale
Airfix Saturn 1b rocket – 1:144 scale
Airfix Bismarck – 1:600 scale
Airfix B-29 – 1:72 scale

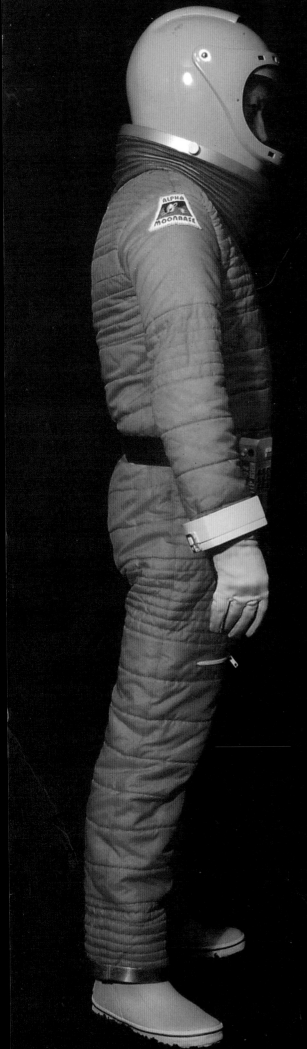

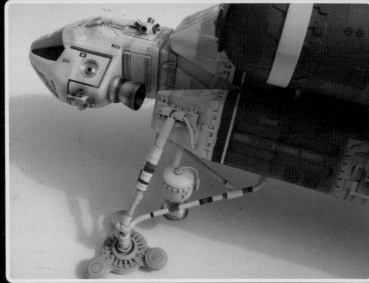

happy medium press
£8.99
ISBN: 978-0-9930320-9-7

9 780993 032097

Airfix Vostok rocket – 1:144 scale
Airfix Lunar Module – 1:72 scale
Airfix SRN4 Hovercraft – 1:144 scale
Airfix/Dapol Travelling Dockside Crane
Ratio 478 Pratt Truss Gantry
Tamiya Matilda MKII tank – 1:35 scale
Revell Gemini Capsule – 1:24 scale

Also required is a Kenworth 1:25 scale lorry kit... I was using a Ford Louisville Hauler, which was very close, before

being given the correct parts. Unfortunately you need multiples of some of these kits, which obviously made my job a lot worse as I was building two Hawks at that time. In the end I got all the kits except for the Matilda, making this an expensive build.

I started by assembling the rear section of the main hull, the sides of which are made from two halves of the Airfix Saturn

V rocket, and cutting out plasticard bulkheads to hold them the correct distance apart. I ran a brass tube down the centre that would later help strengthen the rear engine assembly and create a mounting point for a stand when the model was finished. The roof piece is added later and is a 5cm wide sheet of plasticard. The forward hull is made from a similar mix of plastic sheeting and hull halves, this time using the Airfix Saturn

1b. To do this I made a strong plastic sheet box-section core and then glued the plastic kit parts to its sides. On my original builds the *Saturn 1b* was not available and I had to take an old kit, dismantle it, and then make moulds to cast the multiple parts out of fibreglass resin and car filler mixture.

With the hull now in shape it was detailed with various layers of plastic sheeting, and there's a fair bit of it. Layer on top of layer, with thin ½" strips running down the angled sides covered with rows of small 10mm x 16mm rectangles, and above those thin strips of plastic with dozens of tiny square and rectangular openings cut into the sides – which was almost all invisible on screen and in most publicity photographs!

Having the original model on my workbench for a month meant that a great deal of the initial work could be carried out without the usual time consuming process of drawing plans or doing hundreds of calculations based on photographs. Progress was obviously very much faster than normal.

Sometime in the past I had heard a story that the two long side boosters were made by rolling and gluing plastic sheeting around cardboard kitchen roll tubes. I'm not sure if that's true but the dimensions actually matched my kitchen rolls and the original model certainly uses the rolled plastic sheet technique. When I originally tried to build a *Hawk* I assumed that I would find some 'proper' plastic tubes to use rather than mess about trying to roll thin plastic into something that would not be perfectly round. But the more I thought about it the more I realised that the imperfect rolled method gave a markedly

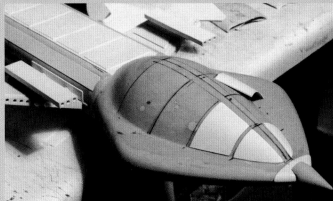

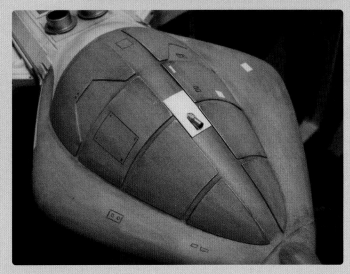

builds, and would do so again even if I had the proper size tube on the shelf.

The boosters are fixed to the main hull along the bottom using two sheets of .060" (1.5mm) *plasticard*, shaped to match up to the contours of the *Saturn V* parts. A small section of framework across the top, made from 1/8th diameter plastic tube, locks everything into place. These parts can now be detailed, which again means more plastic sheet and kit parts... here the *Airfix* 1/72 scale *Lunar Module* comes into play with the most noticeable parts being two rows of the circular footpads glued to 15mm by 42mm panels, two rows of the main landing leg struts (which will always break off at some point in the model's life) and those small attitude thrusters that will always catch on your clothing and snap off!

The front of the boosters have a unique look, with the ends narrowing but also having part of the side cutaway and flattened. On the original studio model

different look to any smooth plastic tube. So I've done that myself on all my *Hawk*

these are just painted wooden parts that appear to have been quickly carved by hand, and as a result they are slightly different on either side. I didn't want to do this myself, especially as I was building two models at that stage, so I decided to just build one example in plastic, make moulds and cast the final parts in a car filler/resin mixture, which could then be reshaped with a little wet and dry paper. These parts also get the kit part and plastic sheet detailing, although what I originally thought was just sheet on the very end is actually a bulkhead kit part from the *Airfix Harrier* that has been cut in half.

Moving to the back we have a rear bulkhead that is covered with kit parts, mostly six very obvious 1:144 scale *Lunar Module* halves – and I always run out of kit parts here and have to cast duplicates. To this panel is attached the main engine with the first section formed entirely from *Saturn V* kit parts. It should be pointed out here that this piece is not exactly in the centre, but positioned slightly higher up.

Although a lot of the model is quite a straightforward build of things that you can just go out and buy (kit parts and plastic sheeting) there are a few problem areas including the nosecone and engine nozzles. The big main engine on the original model was made from part of a wedding cake stand, a *Saturn V* kit piece and part of a *Caddymatic* tea dispenser detailed with a fuel supply pipe formed in filler. Getting this part wrong would ruin the look of the model but there was no easy way of taking a mould off the original model. In the end I did manage to take two plaster moulds off either side of the detailed rear piece of the engine bell. From these I generated copies of both sides and assembled them on a plastic base correcting any faults and filling holes where the parts joined. The kit part was then glued to this, its open end blanked off with plastic, and then a rubber mould was taken. To help the rubber retain its correct shape *Plaster-of-Paris* was poured over the mould to create a support jacket.

The final engine bell part could now be slush-moulded using a mixture of car filler and resin; this was reasonably thin-walled to allow for a heat-moulded internal plastic dome to be added which gives the bell its smooth lining.

The other engine bells were slightly easier to do, especially as the small vertical nozzles are actually plastic vents from an old mattress, and I just happened to have them on a mattress in my spare bedroom! The bells for the two side boosters appear to be made from a plastic cap from an unknown household item, as there are four locking bulges on the inner edge. Luckily I could get a rubber mould off one of the originals but unfortunately I then had a problem with this mould and the cast I got out of it was defective. With the original model now sold I had to repair this casting and use it to generate a new mould, making the parts second generation copies.

Building a *Hawk* nosecone from scratch would also have been a long process, involving time I didn't have, so again I decided to try and take moulds from the original. Obviously I didn't want to damage the delicate model so I carefully covered the nosecone in a layer of kitchen (tin) foil, and then covered that in a backing layer of *Plaster-of-Paris*. From these crude moulds I generated almost solid copies in car filler that I could then sand down to match the original's shape, thus creating a set of master patterns. I also made a duplicate cast of the lower centre bulge to use for vac-forming the plastic panel cladding later.

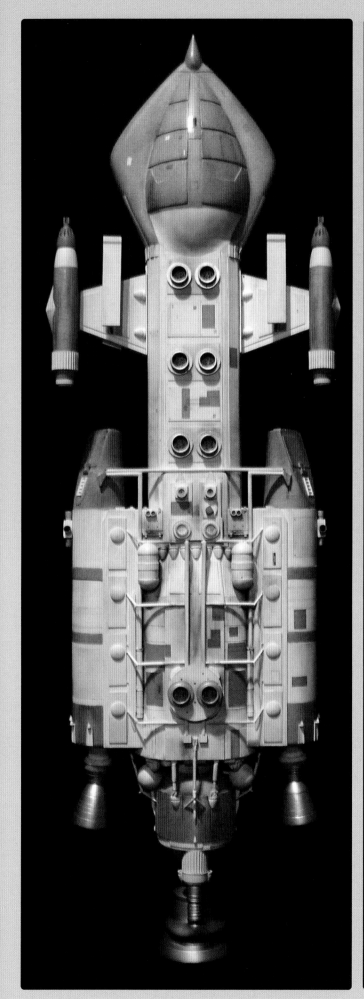

Fibreglass nosecones were now cast up from plaster moulds, and then the two window areas drilled out and filed to shape. To form these areas I used thick *plasticard* for the horizontal pieces, and filler for the vertical ones. Unlike the *Eagle Transporter* the horizontal parts are recessed into the hull (which caught me out on my first build twenty-five years ago) creating a lip that runs around the edges, starting at around 2mm near the windows to 3mm at the nose. There are also slight lips on the vertical centrepiece, but I don't think that they are intentional so I made mine flush.

The nosecone halves were superglued together then attached to the main body with screws and filler. On the original model there is a very visible join line covered on either side with a series of small plastic pieces (10mm x 4mm sized, with 8 on the left side and 9 on the right). I decided to make the join a little

less obvious and so it is mostly just a slight indentation and weathered line on my replicas.

Whilst I had access to the original model I had traced a number of the panel outlines onto paper. These could now be cut out and used as templates to cut new *plasticard* panels. I had feared that I might have to heat-form the panels on the top of the cabin but as the plastic is quite thin I could just use standard flat sheet. The panels on the big lower bulge definitely needed to be heat-formed to the correct shape before I could cut them out and glue them into place. I had to carefully draw out the positions on the lower hull to get everything perfectly in line with the correct spacing – which seemed slightly strange as the nosecone is so unsymmetrical and out of shape itself.

The windows themselves are just made from yellow tinted clear plastic sheeting. I know that some modellers add pilots, a

detailed interior, and even lights occasionally, but I never considered any of this as my aim was simply to build a copy of the original studio model. Also, you never see any of that in the episode, and as the *Hawks* were actually just supposed to be illusions created by aliens then they wouldn't actually contain human pilots.

The spine is only window dressing on the *Hawk* and is just glued into place. It is basically two long 3/16" diameter brass pipes with 1/8" cross beams.

The solar panel was again just made from layers of *plasticard*. Apparently the original piece was a footpad from another model that had been turned over, which explains why it has so much detail on the underside.

The front weapon pods are mostly made of *Airfix Harrier* kit parts; the ribbed section, however, is just a section of tubing from a wedding cake stand. The pieces aren't actually wide enough and have to be split on the sides facing the hull, small 5mm wide pieces of plastic cover the gaps. The mini-wings themselves are simply made by gluing four layers of .060" (1.5mm) *plasticard* together.

The big issue when it comes to the *Hawk* is its colour scheme and I wasn't sure which one I was going to use until the very end of the build. As you may know (or possibly not) the *Hawk* was originally delivered to the studio and initially filmed in a basic white finish with black window surrounds. As this was then considered to be too 'Eagle-like' it was quickly given new orange highlights and white window surrounds. Sometime after filming the window surrounds were then given a new black finish, making it the *Hawk's* third colour scheme, and it has remained that way for the last forty-plus years.

Personally I would have liked the *Hawk* much better if it had remained in its original guise, so I seriously considered painting mine all white but finally went with the orange look. As I have also become so familiar with seeing the *Hawk* sporting black window surrounds I have rather naturally tended to hate the white-look and fully intended to paint mine black. However, while the model was still mostly in its primer stage I began to think it actually looked rather smart and so the replica featured here does indeed resemble the 'as-filmed' version from the episode.

But since completing that model I have seen the *Hawk* pictured in the workshop at Bray Studios during the second series of **Space: 1999** and it had the black window surrounds again, so my current (and last) *Hawk* build is finally going to have the black look.

Basic paint finish consisted of matt white motorcar spray primer and hand-painted *Humbrol No. 18 Gloss Orange*, with a final coat of clear matt varnish. Many **1999** modellers have used this paint over the years, but there is now the suggestion that the model maker at the studio may have used an artist's paint like *Cadmium Deep Yellow* gouache, so I'll be trying that next time.

One minor colour alteration was to slightly lighten the blue-tipped weapon pods so they stand out better against the dark space backgrounds. Weathering included rubbing over the orange paint with fine wet and dry paper to give it a nice scuffed look. As I'm so used to seeing the present day grubbier appearance of the original model I dirtied down my copy far more than it appeared in the series; although the weathered look didn't seem to work on the window surrounds so I've left them pristine white!

The *Hawk* isn't what I would call one of my 'better builds', and that's actually intentional. The original model was built quickly and has a roughness that I wanted to capture in my replica. That's why I copied the nosecone that is actually very lopsided with the windows pointing more to the left than directly forwards. I also used the rolled plastic sheet for the booster tubes, added detail to just one side of the solar panel, and only used silver paint on the engine bells instead of some fancy chrome paint ...basically walking the fine line of building a good model while trying not to make it appear 'too good'. Because to me that roughness adds a substantial feeling to the *Hawk* that compliments its aggressive nature, with its unsymmetrical cabin giving it the appearance of a broken-nosed boxer who has had too many bouts but is still looking for his next fight! The *Hawk's* a bad boy, and shouldn't look too neat and pretty.

More of David's superb model making can be seen at:
www.davidsissonmodels.co.uk/

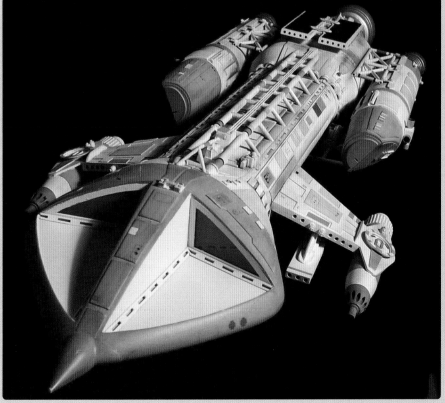

Man had recently walked on the Moon and SF TV programmes of the time gave viewers a taste of things to come. Us kids of that first decade of the seventies felt we actually were viewing the future. The truth is we were seeing through a telescope... from the wrong side...

As with most TV and movie science fiction presentations, authors, artists and producers never have in mind to depict exactly what is going to happen in the future, their intention being to simply bring us *fun*... just *fun*. This is because the technology depicted in such programmes becomes obsolete within just a few years from the date when the series first airs. In the case of **Space: 1999**, the *Stun Gun* has

yet to be invented (the problem is how on earth do you store enough energy to be able to fire a hand-held laser), and the *Comlock* can be compared to a contemporary TV remote control incorporating a small viewing screen (as is well known, a real monitor screen was used on the 'hero' *Comlock* and this prop was a little bigger than the standard one because it needed to house the smallest screen electronics had to offer at the time).

Stun Gun

Among sci-fi space pistols, the *Stun Gun* is one of my favourites (along with the **Star Trek TOS** *Phaser*), even though it does somewhat resemble a stapler, as everyone points out. Perhaps production designer Keith Wilson looked to *Dan Dare*'s '50s-

style gun for inspiration, as this features a somewhat similar design with the addition of a barrel (and kind of looks like a WW2 *Mauser*).

For some reason, as viewers needed to quickly understand if a victim was to be killed or simply stunned, a two-view device was added to the top of the *Gun* (*mark II*), transforming a very graceful

Recreating the technology of the future

Jean-Marc Deschamps scratchbuilds replica Stun Gun and Comlock props

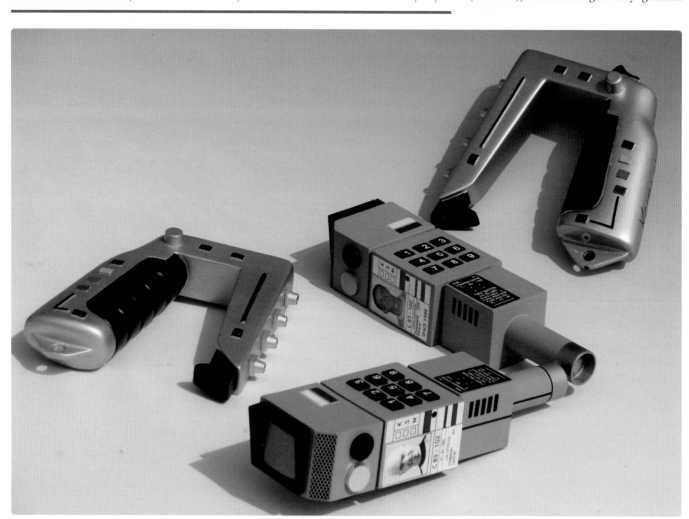

LES DERNIERS GARDIENS DE LA PLANETE MAHRA 2

TOUJOURS PRÊT! TOUJOURS PLEIN!

PUISSANT

Son réservoir grande contenance lui donne une puissance permettant d'atteindre plusieurs mètres.

PRÉCIS

Son mécanisme de pompe à dépression, lui permet de concentrer le jet de façon précise. Il ne rate jamais sa cible.

RÉARMABLE

D'un coup sec du poignet vers l'arrière, tu mets en service la réserve de "munitions".

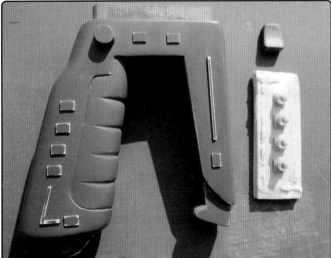

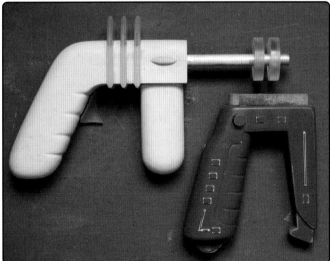

Opposite and top left: Poster of French magazine *Pif Super Gadget* with kids outfitted as UFO characters! Top right: Inside the water pistol *Stun Gun!* Above and left: Master of the *Stun Gun* made of *Lab* . The wood block at the top is for casting purposes. Right: Comparison between two SF gun masters—*Dan Dare* and **Space:1999**. Above: 'nozzles' cast in resin.

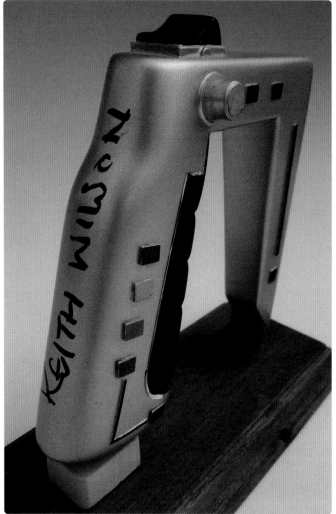

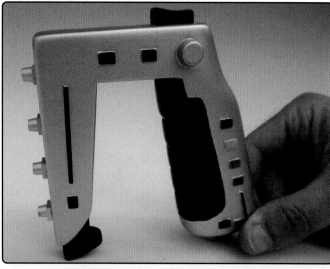

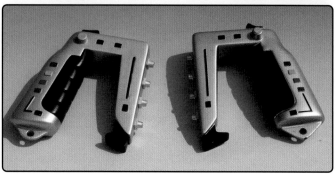

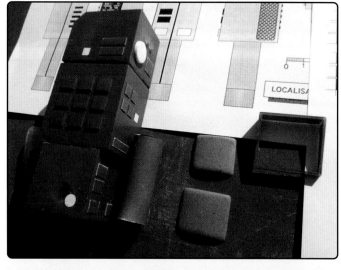

Top: Completed *Stun Gun*. Left and above: *Perspex* master with different plans and two sizes of screen. Opposite top left: Assembled and primed *Comlock*. Opposite top right and inset: Two renditions of the same *Comlock* – with and without black stripes.

piece of technological design into a clunky mechanical gadget far removed from the future we all dreamed of. For that reason, I preferred to not incorporate the 'mode selector' feature into my recreation.

A great many *Stun Gun* props were created during production of the series. Some were better than others (those appearing in the foreground of scenes) although most of them were crudely made from vacform shells and quickly painted, resulting in variants in terms of shape and making it difficult to find something I could

use as a starting point for my build. Luckily – and strangely – a French kids' magazine, well known in France for spotlighting a 'gadget' in each issue, published a new edition called *Pif Super Gadget* (*Pif* being the name of the hero dog character and the familiar French name for the nose). This was around 1981 and the featured 'super gadget' in this issue was a water pistol called the *Arm Master*, which was nothing more than the famous **Space: 1999** *Stun Gun*! Of course this was only a toy for kids, but with some surgical interventions I managed to transform it into an acceptable reproduction of my favourite pistol – one which series production designer Keith Wilson and series star Barry Morse, met during conventions in France, subsequently signed.

I wanted a more decent replica of the *Stun Gun*, however, and in the late eighties, armed with photographs sourced from various books and magazines (*Starlog*, *Starlog Special Weapons*, and the very good *Supermarionation Is Go* magazines), I was able to draw plans onto cardboard to judge of the size of the gun then transfer these onto a block of *Lab*, which is a synthetic material (some kind of hard resin) which can be cut (with an electric saw) and carved. Raised details were created from *Evergreen* plastic profiles. The trigger was made of the same

material and all the nozzles were cast from a *Perspex* tube turned on a lathe, the four castings being glued on top of different thicknesses of squares of plastic to be cast again. My *Stun Gun* master, fully primed, was ready to be moulded to produce a few castings. I painted my own gun silver and masked the areas where the coloured 'buttons' are (*Weapons Manuel* author Shane Johnson, in an article published decades ago, stated: *red* is for Power on/off, *yellow* for Low Intensity, *green* for High Intensity and *blue* for Infrared. The big conical caps at the top to each side of the gun are for the Safety. ... All of which is fine...unless the user happens to be colour-blind).

At the beginning of the nineties, an American guy called John F. Green, who specialised in vintage SF kits, asked me if I would sell him some *Stun Gun* kits, which I did. Soon after, Tony James from *Comet Miniatures*, well know for his Aladdin's Cave of exclusive kits, also asked me the same thing. At that time he was selling a 22" resin and metal kit of the *Eagle* I was looking for (the *Eagle* is one of my favourite subjects too). We struck a deal: he would send me the *Eagle* kit, I would provide him with my *Stun Gun* kits. Today there are a great many different *Stun Gun* kits available, all with different shapes, but over the years mine has been cited as one of the rarest, most sought after replicas, and I am proud of that.

Comlock

By the middle of the nineties my *Stun Gun* was looking a bit lonely and I therefore decided to create an infernal machine... sorry... a *companion*, for it. It was time to built the famous *Comlock*, sometimes spelled as *Comlock* with one 'M', and sometimes as *Commlock*, with two (I even remember having seen it written with three 'M's when viewing the series on videotape!). Many plans of the prop can be found and they are, of collision-course, all different. One of these, however, (signed D. Schreiner) seemed accurate enough by comparison to my documents. Here the build was easier because the *Comlock* is composed mostly of flat surfaces that can be built up directly from sheets of plastic or *Perspex* (I prefer the latter material). The raised details are *Evergreen* and all the markings (including numbers and technical specifications) were drawn on a computer and printed onto thick paper. I even used a photograph of *Commander* 'two M's' *Koenig*, over which I stuck my face.

The *Comlock* masters were then seamlessly cast in resin by a friend and painted a standard grey... yes – just 'grey' (not even *Ford Polar Grey* that is just for space tourists! My friend Olivier used a different grey for his *Comlock*) before adding colour to the specific details. Numbers and other markings were glued in place and sealed. Finally, I chose to paint the screen silver with a blue hue to simulate the look of a TV screen.

...End communication.

Quest for perfection

David Pearson enhances Round 2's Moonbase Alpha
reissue and rebuilds Imai's Eagle kit.

Building a better base

When *Round 2* reintroduced the old *Moonbase Alpha* kit I just had to try my hand at building it with a new twist. They had improved the layout of the base, with five correctly scaled pads (and *Eagles*) instead of the three from previous releases, and this time the lunar terrain had better detail, although still made from flimsy, vacuum-formed plastic. *Problem one:* how do I make the base more rigid and strong? Also, the *Main Mission* part was left uncorrected with the same inaccurate small office, inaccurate staircase and *Kano*'s desk missing. *Problem two:* how do I modify or scratchbuild elements to properly represent the Office, and add corrected and missing elements to the Operations Area?

The first issue addressed with the base was finding a way to make the plastic more rigid, so that parts would not fall off due to flexing. Initially I tried spray foam, but that proved problematic by distorting the thin plastic, then strips of wood from a craft store in two sizes, 3/8" square and 3/16" x 3/8". The thicker strip was used along the outer edges, then through the centre diagonally to each corner. The thinner 3/16" x 3/8" strips were placed at 90 degree angles to the larger strips

through the centre, then connected midway to the larger strips along the outer edge. The assembly was glued in place with CA, using shims made from the strips to support gaps underneath the lunar terrain. Sheet plastic, .020 thick, was CA'd in place over the bottom to finish the assembly, which is still lightweight but much more strong and rigid [1-2].

After addressing gaps between buildings and the base surface with sheet plastic shims and making the seams between panels blend in, building and *Travel Tube* locations were masked off to avoid the need to remove paint when gluing them in place. I then sprayed the base with a 50/50 mixture of *Model Master Enamel Neutral Gray* and *Lt. Ghost Gray*. All the old *Travel Tube* locations on all buildings were covered over with thin strip plastic, .010 thick at the appropriate width, to create nicer joining surfaces with the new *Travel Tubes*. Random panels on all buildings and *Launch Pads* were brush painted with *Model Master Lt. Gray*, and all these parts were airbrushed *Flat White* with a few light coats for blending [3-4]. *Travel Tubes* and *Eagles* were handled in the same way: *Lt. Gray* first followed by light coats of *Flat White*. Buildings, *Launch Pads* and *Travel Tubes* received

some extra definition with line work lightly applied with a fine tip pencil. Small black squares were added as windows to buildings and *Launch Pads* [A], these coming from a 12" *Eagle* decal sheet reduced to 66% and being placed randomly in groups of two, three and four, stacked two high in some places. After the *Pad* decals were added the base was lightly washed with black acrylic. For any small gaps between building bottoms and the lunar surface I used canopy glue retouched with base colour. I then drybrushed a lighter shade of the base colour over parts of the lunar terrain. The buildings, *Pads* and *Tubes* were installed at this point, and flat clear airbrushed over the entire base to knock down any shiny spots, *Eagles* being installed last because of silver painted engine bells [B-D].

The second issue with this kit is recreating the Office more accurately and correcting and adding missing detail to *Main Mission's* Operations Area. Before starting modifications, consult reference sources like the *Catacombs* website to become familiar with the set layout. Making a more accurate Office floor requires a second kit for the extra Operations Area floor – you need to cut

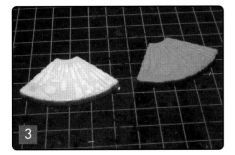

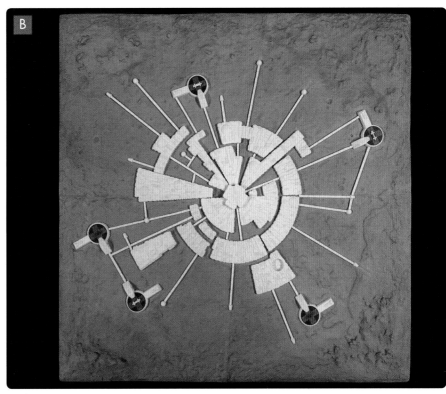

the second Operations floor away as well as the raised platform where the computer wall is located, and mirror the parts to become the Office floor [5]. Where the steps meet the walls, partial walls were created out of sheet plastic, cut to the same height as the raised platforms – one at the side outer wall ¾" long, and one at the back 'viewer' wall 5/8" long. The tops of these, where the floor extends out to meet them, can be filled in with extra pieces of stock floor or thick sheet plastic. Also, I created small walls where the steps meet the raised platforms and partial walls. The inner, Office wall where the two doorways are located was formed using two separate wall segments from the stock kit Office: the back wall and a side wall. These were carefully lined up and joined together to appear as one continuous wall [6].

It was now time to locate where the two doorways would be, using the old *Starlog Technical Notebook Main Mission* plan – I know this isn't accurate, but it's close enough. I cut out small segments off the horizontal, mid wall, raised frame and also used a standing kit figure to judge the width as well as height of the doors. The door frames were constructed from *Evergreen* .030 x .020 strip ...don't forget the vertical nubs at the tops of both door frames!

Now the fun began: the Office back wall was scratchbuilt [8] from .030 sheet plastic and the plastic strips needed to replicate the vertical and horizontal frames gauged from the kit parts, as was the spacing between them. If memory serves, the bottom 'baseboard' is .030 x .020 strip, and all others .040 x .020 strip. A word about where the corners of the walls meet: all wall corners end with vertical frames that need to come together neatly – you should have a 1/16" flange or lip at the end of each wall. The outer Office wall [9-10] – yep, the one with the windows, is pieced together from the extra Operations window wall and an extra Office side wall.

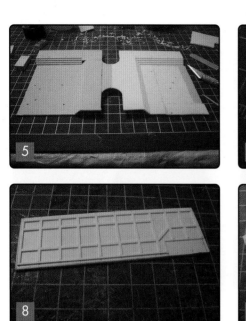

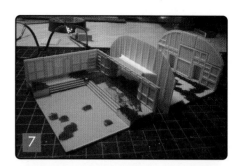

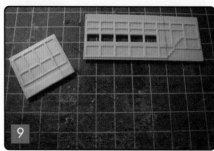

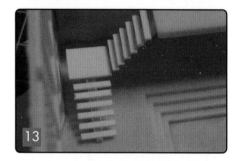

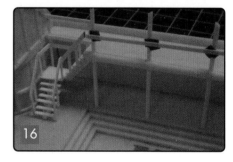

Cut-offs at each wall end are shown with pencil line. The Office side wall is to the left of the windows, and the cut line on the right becomes the new corner. For joining, the key here is to line up both top horizontal frames and thicken the join line with strip so it matches the thickness of the horizontal frame below the windows. You need to add strip to the top of the Office side wall segment so it matches the top edge of the window wall, and remove the top horizontal frame without reducing the height of the joining vertical frames, just removing the middle horizontal segments. After the segments are removed, add .040 x .020 strip along the tops of the vertical frames. Add thin strip to the right of the windows to become the new corner, remove the last centre, right horizontal frame from the Office side wall, and add the diagonal strip, lining up as pictured. Also, you need to remove some material at

the lower right edge of the Office side wall, at the join line, so the raised floor and partial wall will fit. Last note about this outer Office wall: I filled in the fifth window towards the corner, but the accurate configuration is *three* Office windows, so the choice is up to the builder. The forth Office wall, or entry wall, is simply the entry wall to the Operations Area reversed with the top part removed, and where they come together on both curved sides I added strip to space them apart for a better floor fit, this also suggesting opened sliding doors. I also suggested shelves in the corners where this entry wall meets the side walls with .030 x .020 strip.

Final notes about the floor in both areas: locator holes were filled with rod and CA. The conference table [18] for the Office was made from a small plastic

medicine bottle, an end carefully cut off, sanded to the right thickness, and filled in the centre with sheet plastic and putty. The table base is tube and squares of sheet plastic, .010 thick, dimensions based on a seated kit figure. The smaller table is similar to the conference table, but because of its smaller size, tube was used for the top, filled in with smaller tubing and putty, with a base made from the same. Couches were created from .030 sheet plastic for the seat and backrest, with arms made from .020 sheet plastic, again using a seated figure for sizing. The Communication Post was a 3/32" square piece of wood covered with thin sheet plastic, plastic rod and a small square of sheet plastic making up the base.

A new, larger Office ceiling grid is needed, so based on the size and spacing of the kit part, I created one from .060

square strip. A note about how the grid fits, or rests, on the top edge of the walls: you need to create a lip, like those on the stock kit walls, for the scratchbuilt back, inner and outer sides and modified entry walls. The new grid will slide in place and rest on the top of the horizontal wall frames.

Next up, scratchbuilding new stairs for the Operations Area. Start with .010 plastic strips at about 1/8" wide, 1 inch long, and angled at 45 degrees. You need four of these, two per flight of steps, and need to cut 'teeth' on the top edge, 1/16" high and deep. Now sandwich a piece of .060 square strip, 1 inch in length, with the two before-mentioned strips making sure the teeth are above the square strip. Then set up a little rig where the part will be at a 45 degree angle and cut .020 x .060 strips into 11/32" segments – the steps. Cut six of these per flight, then, using plastic cement, glue one on at a time making sure they are level, square and centred to each other. When making both flights, make two sets of eight teeth. The first and last teeth don't receive steps, just the six in between. The ends of the part will become mating surfaces for the balcony to the landing, or landing to floor. Cut a 3/8" square of .020 sheet plastic to become the landing, and cut a new interface at the balcony at approximately 3/8" x 7/8". One at a time, CA glue each flight to the landing, remembering to check the parts are square, even and centered, while maintaining the 45 degree angles. When both flights are glued to the landing, glue the assembly to the balcony making sure all relationships are proper yet again! With this done it's time to make some

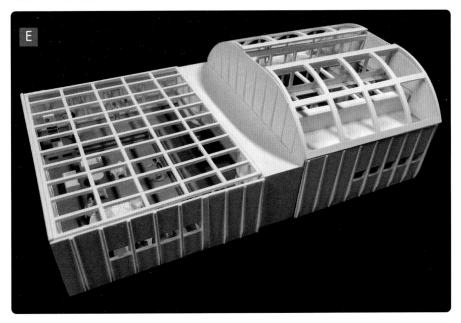

railings. Vertical supports are .030 x .020 strip, and rails .040 x .020 strip. Make a 45 degree angle rig on a piece of masking tape so you can cut the proper angle. Make the rails one section, or flight, at a time, then, starting with the outside railing, work your way up to the balcony level. For this to look right, constantly look at your relationships and take your time – the railing will connect to the bottom of the balcony on the backside of flight number two. The longer cut edge at the balcony, or interface, may need building out with some strip to get it to align with the railing. I recommend scratchbuilding new balcony supports and railing, so it matches the new staircase, and lines up as well. I drilled new holes in the balcony and the floor below because I wanted the tops of the supports to end under the kit-supplied ceiling grid! I made a template of the new balcony holes, then transferred this to the floor below. To help in getting your balcony railing established, use a kit figure for height, then start building the inner railing for the staircase like the outside railing. You'll also want to add a partial balcony railing at the backside of the upper flight of steps matching the height of the main balcony railing. Take your time and be patient – eveything will come together! [11-16]

The next modification, *Kano*'s desk, [17] was made from the extra set of work consoles – cut one of the smaller kit consoles free and thicken the outer edge with some strip. OK, that's the top part – now you need to scratchbuild the support frame. Referencing the height of the kit-supplied consoles, build your frame from .030 x .020 strip, using the masking tape trick to get your angles and alignments right. The turntable it sits on is a 5/8" round piece of .020 plastic, this time cut from the sheet with the edge carefully sanded. To allow this to fit between the other consoles, the main console needs to be widened a bit – I used a sized piece of .030 plastic glued at the centre after it was carefully cut apart. The final things on the construction list are the shroud and covers for the bottoms of raised step areas along the outer walls. The shroud is .020 sheet plastic cut to size and fits between the two entry walls as a cosmetic feature. The covers at the raised step areas are made from the same sheet plastic, cut to fit as well. The paint menu is as follows: all *Model Master Enamel* colours, *Lt. Ghost Gray* for the floor, a mixture of *Sand* and *Flat White* for the walls, twenty drops of *Sand* per half ounce of *Flat White*.

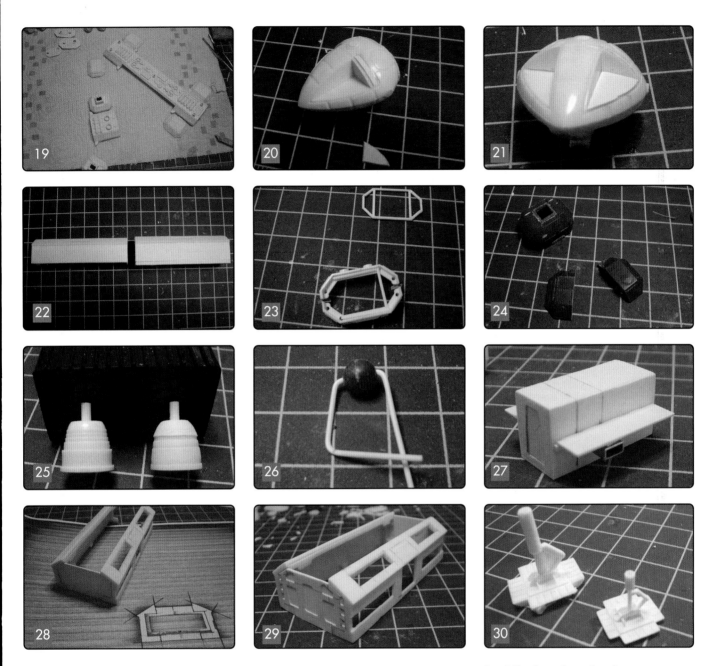

Consoles are *Neutral Gray*, same with the Commander's Desk, but sides and legs are silver; all chairs, couches, and Office tables are *Flat White*. Overall uniform colour for figures is three parts *Flat White* to one part *Sand*. Referencing the *Catacombs* again, I picked out and masked light panels on walls to be sprayed *Gloss White*. I copied the kit-supplied decals to use separate bits, from the computer wall decal, to detail the Communication Post. The 'C' at the top of the Post I made, the instrument panels at the side office doors are also cut up spares. The Viewscreen on the back office wall is just a resized version of the Main Viewer with detail at top and bottom handled like the Communication Post. I used plain white decal material for the raised step area vertical surfaces, with grey rectangular bits from the extra decal sheet. The instrument decals on the

consoles seemed flat and uninteresting, so I picked out lights here and there with different paint colours via a fine tip brush. I also used a fine tip pencil to pick out moulded details on the consoles. With straight edge and template, conference table details were carefully drawn with a fine tip pencil.

In wrapping up this project, I not only built an accurate and strong *Alpha*, but also, with elbow grease, achieved a more accurate *Main Mission* [F-I]. The Office, even though corrected, is on the large side – the actual set was proportionally smaller, but looks much better than an out of the box build! Projects like this take lots of patience and work, but certainly help increase a modeller's skill level. Thanks to all at *Round 2 Models* for re-popping this cool little kit!

Imai Eagle reimagined

Inspiration for this project began in 2001. After seeing the wonderfully modified *AMT/Ertl Eagles* on *Small Art Works'* website, I decided to purchase an *AMT* kit for my own modified build. Thought I'd found one online, but when I received the model it was the very crude Japanese *Imai* kit – the vendor hadn't replaced the image of the *AMT* kit with the *Imai* version [19]. *AUGH!* At first I wanted to return it, but then decided to give it a go and modify the thing as best as I could, even though it was worse than the *AMT* version. The project took months to complete, but when finished it was a model I was proud to display for years until it was sold to a friend, Gordon Morriguchi. He purchased the model via *eBay*, but it was unfortunately lost by the Post Office. What to do!? I had a second model in my stash of an earlier version of the *Imai* kit

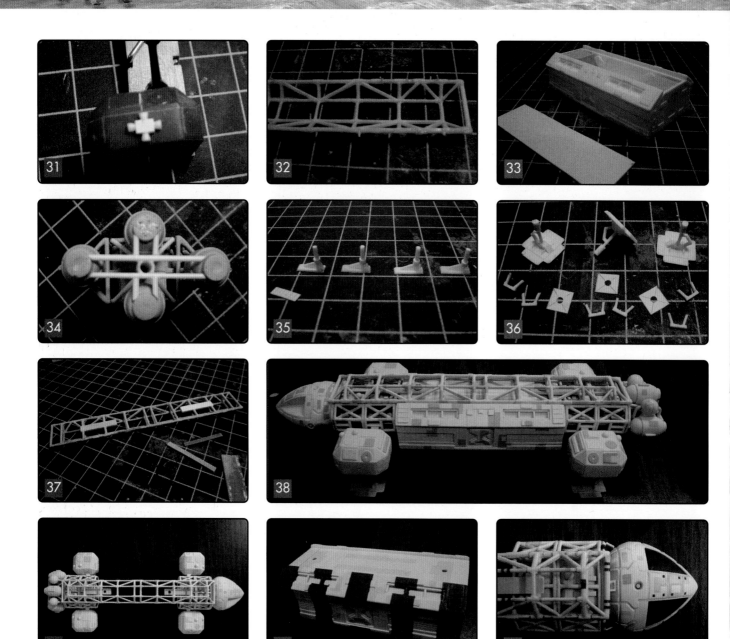

and decided to give it another go, this time modifying and scratchbuilding the parts with better detail. I then made RTV moulds to cast multiple parts to recreate the lost *Eagle*. Lastly, this replacement was cleaned up, assembled and finished... This was the first time I had basically created my own kit, and it was my first completed all-resin kit...

...My second trip down this road began with the same type modifications and scratchbuilding. Work began on the second kit by separating parts to be modified and stripping paint, then it was time to narrow the spine and scratchbuild a more accurate cage assembly with interior module. The beauty of the modular *Eagle* design is repetition of parts, so one or two moulds equals multiple parts. By using one stock *Cage* structure from the kit, spaced at the centre

by 3/64", I made the end frames for the *Cages* out of *Evergreen* 3/64" plastic rod stock [23]. Rod spacers, with the same size rod stock, were cut to 15/32" lengths and joined to the completed end frames using a form made of sheet plastic. Later the cross details were added. The inside *Cage Module* was made of sheet plastic to overall dimensions ½" wide, 9/16" high, and 1 and 3/32" long. The shelves at either side are 1" long x ¼" wide; the sockets for the *Shoulder Pods* were made from *K&S* brass stock, 3/32" x 3/16" rectangular bar tube cut at 1 and 1/16" length [27]. The final *Cage Module* was detailed with *Evergreen* rod, tube, half round, and strip stock. I then began *Command Module* modifications by filling in the insets for the cockpit windows with various thicknesses of sheet plastic. Actual window surfaces were built out by 7/64", the horizontal sections,

upper and lower, needing angled build up as well – in the stock kit, they're flat [20-21]. The height of the *CM* was reduced by sanding down the inside edges of each half. The joining plate from the kit used to mount the *CM* was glued in place at the back and rounded to shape. After filling in the original sensor dishes at top and bottom, revised dishes were carefully located and cut with a 3/32" drill. The *Passenger Pod* saw the inaccurate details sanded off [22], the height of the structure was reduced by 3/32" and 3/16" was removed from the centre join line.

Modifications of the *Pod* side began with locating, marking, and removing material [28-29] where correct details would be added – openings for the windows are 3/16" x 13/16" and the frames are made from .030 x .040 strip. The door is ½" x 15/32", and the insets at

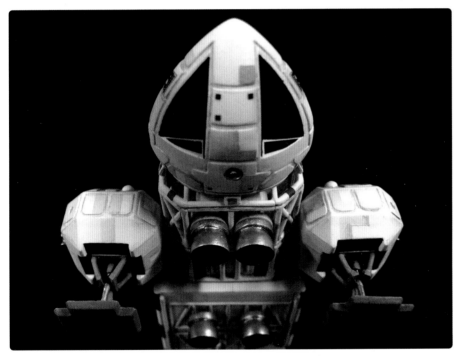

either side are 13/64" x 1 and 1/32". The door is detailed with .010 and .020 sheet plastic and the inset detail is *Evergreen* HO scale car siding. A correct *Pod* end wall was made using .010 and .020 sheet plastic and cut to shape using a pattern photocopied from the joined side walls. A new *Passenger Pod* bottom was made from .020 sheet and detailed with .040 half round. Feet were made from rod, tube, strip and sheet plastic [35]. The stock engine tanks from the kit are moulded together, so were cut apart, and the more complete tanks modified with rod and tube stock. Two of the smaller round tanks [26] had holes cut through their centres and were joined by 3/64" rod in a rectangular formation with the dimensions of ½" x 11/16". A main engine bell from the kit was modified using strip and tubing stock [25] and the vertical, take off and landing bell, that would become many, was scratchbuilt from two sizes of tubing stock, 5/16" and ¼". Transitions between tubing sizes were smoothed with filler putty. *Shoulder Pod* modifications [24] began by cutting a section out of the middles of two, about a 1/16", and removing the box structures at the bottoms, resulting holes being filled in with sheet plastic. Details were added using rounded kit sprues and thicker sheet plastic, .030, was cut in strips and used for mounting arms. The quad thruster for the *Shoulder Pods* [31] was made from thicker sheet plastic with filed and shaped 1/16" rod stock for nozzles. The kit's basic landing foot was thickened with .020 sheet plastic and reshaped, the attaching strut being scratchbuilt from 3/64" rod, 3/32" tube, strip for the scissor, and thin sheet plastic with scribed 'toes'. The brackets that attach the assembly to the *Shoulder Pod* bottoms were made from tube and strip [36].

The next step was to create RTV moulds of the modified and scratchbuilt parts. Being new to moulds and casting resin parts there was some trial and error to overcome. For example, adding more detail to the master parts seemed to cause more bubbles on the final resin parts. Also, mould set up was problematic at first, so simplifications and the introduction of pour tabs to get bubbles out of the moulds became necessary. Even improved mould set up and pouring still yielded some bubbles, so repairs to cast parts couldn't be avoided. As with most modellers, my 'home spun' process was good enough at a certain point, so I had to make the best examples work.

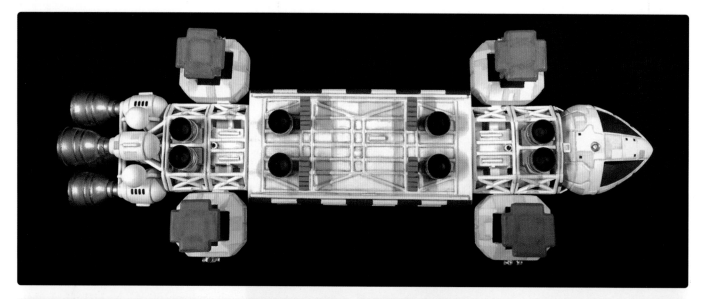

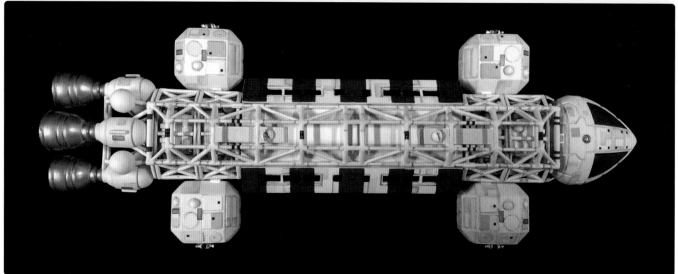

The final step was to clean up, assemble and finish the newly made parts. Work began on the *Spine* [32] and *Cages* to fill in pin holes, the larger holes being filled in with stretched sprue and CA. The *Cage Interior Modules* needed similar repair work, along with the *CM* and *Engine Tanks*. To see if additional repairs were needed, I primed all these parts. Construction then moved to the *Passenger Pod*, and after additional clean-up work all pieces were joined and blocks of wood installed for the mounting screws to secure the *Pod* to the *Spine*. The top of the *Pod* is a plain sheet of .020 plastic [33]. A *CM* mount was made from sheet plastic and a section of 3/32" tube to join it with the forward cage section. The A-frame for the engine section was made using 3/64" rod, cut into four sections at 5/8" lengths, and one 5/32" tube, cut at a 7/8" length. All large *Engine Tanks* are mounted to the rear *Cage* along axis lines, top, bottom, and sides, using small sections of paper clip wire. The *Engine Tank* rear mounts

are also made from 3/64" rod, two horizontal rods at 1" lengths, and four smaller vertical rods at 5/32" lengths, all cut with angled ends [34]. Next, I assembled the *Main Landing Gear* using stretched sprue and CA to fill large holes. Mounting plates for the *Gear* were made from .010 sheet plastic, 5/16" square, and joined with the brackets that attach to the gear tops. Struts for the *Passenger Pod* landing gear were rebuilt with rod and tube stock, and foot pad skids made from scribed sheet plastic.

All *Engine Bells*, including the *Shoulder Pod* quad thrusters, underwent final clean-up and primer application. Next, the mount plates for the *Passenger Pod* were made from .030 sheet plastic and cut into 7/8" x ¼" strips. These were assembled to the lower spine rungs [37], second and third in from each end, then the *Cages* assembled to the *Spine*. After the rest of the parts received primer and got final tweaks, all parts were airbrushed

Model Master Flat White [39] and all *Bells* sprayed *Silver*. The small *Engine Tanks* were joined to the inside centres of both larger side *Tanks*, then all *Tanks* were glued to the *Rear Cage*. After a few more sanding and smoothing tweaks followed by touch-up white paint, the grey panels were airbrushed (and brush painted) to the entire model. With this set, all parts were dusted with *White* via the airbrush to tone down the grey panels.

The always-fun rescue stripes on the *Passenger Pod* [40] were masked with strips of *Scotch* tape at 21/64" widths: five red stripes, and four white, all equal width. *Testors Flat Red* was applied with a brush. More contrasting grey panels were added to the whole model and lighter grey paint added to the 'toes' of the *Main Landing Gear*.

At long last the decal process began: I shrunk down aftermarket decals for a 12" *Eagle* to 66% to achieve the proper size.

After all decals were applied and a flat clear coat sprayed to the entire model, a black acrylic wash was lightly applied around select details for added interest. The entire model was then airbrushed with flat clear once more, and final assembly completed [41].

The end result is an *Eagle* that looks much closer to the originals – by no means perfect, but far better than a stock build! The detail level that can be achieved with this scale *Eagle* opens up display options for fans who have limited space. Since building this second *Eagle* I've completed a third with a lunar base and backdrop, this model being auctioned at a 2014 convention in the UK. I'm currently building six more, three with *Lab Pods* and *Spine Boosters*. All six will have aluminium engine bells, and one of these little 'polished' beauties is *mine*!

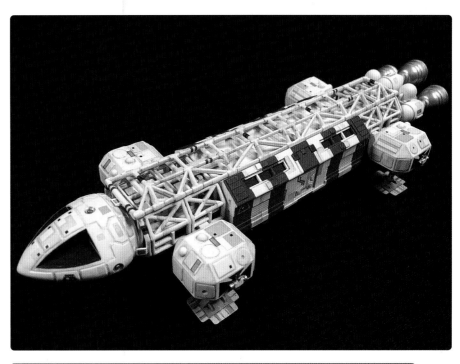

Shots of finished models by: Gordon Moriguchi.

Further examples of Space: 1999 subjects built by David Pearson.

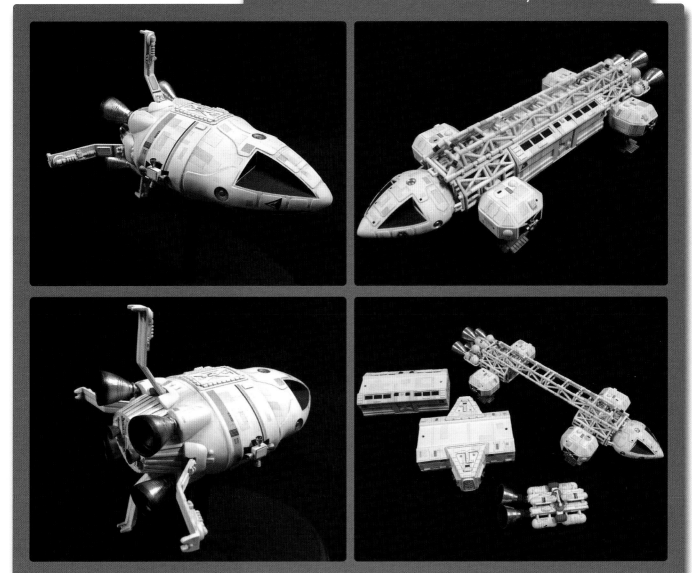

Building a
BIGGER
buggy

A photo-article featuring Chris Rogerson's build of Retro Models' large Moon Buggy kit

...OK, so I get the chance to lay my hands on the 12th scale **Space:1999** *Moon Buggy* kit from *Retro Models*. I am usually worried about what I'll find in a garage kit box... Will it need a pound of filler to get rid of any defects? Will it look like a *Cadbury's Crunchie* bar? Will it be warped and need the hairdryer treatment?

A pleasant surprise awaited: polyester resin that was not sticky and blotchy and a very fine cast indeed! Hats off to Phil Howard at *Retro* for nailing it down!

Laying all the parts out on the bench [1], it was easy to see what goes where and it's all very straightforward. The two halves of the body needed virtually no clean up at all... a nice, solid cast with the footwell for the controls and channeled out for headlight wiring with plenty of space for a battery casing and switch.

Firstly, all the cleanup done, I set about laying down some primer on the main parts [2]. *Halfords'* ever faithful sprays are a god-send for any model maker in the UK, offering a wealth of colours to cater for any model project. The six chunky balloon tyres come complete with steel axles already fitted and it's just a case of a quick rub down before priming. The fixing points are pre-drilled, a nice, snug fit keeps them in place and they can also rotate without coming off.

The instructions are very comprehensive and are in full colour with large pictures to guide you through every step, also giving pointers for the scheme to use on the final

paint run. It's clear from the shots that there were quite a few studio miniatures created to different scales, and for distance/close-up filming, etc. I chose to go with the full size variant, with a page of shots of this being supplied too – great research leaving no stone unturned to give the maker the option to build any version from season one or two.

The colour recommended is *Snapdragon Yellow* and I believe this is an old *British Leyland* shade? I'm sure someone will confirm or deny this at some point. The trek to *Halfords* drew a blank with this, so rather than take the expensive option of having them mix a can I searched online and the nearest colour I could find to it was *Signal Yellow*, being a very close match indeed [3-4].

I painted the two hull halves separately and left them to go off, then it was on to final assembly and weathering.

Some of the folks who have also tackled this kit have used magnets to keep the two pieces together. As this is a static kit in my cabinet, the weight of it alone keeps it from going anywhere and also allows replacement/repair of the battery and light fixtures if required [8]. The decals supplied are very comprehensive too: dashboard controls [7], markings and the various black stripes that adorn the miniature are all included [5-6] and there are also options available of tool and storage boxes and a lunar surface base.

An interesting point in closing... folks who have seen this model have mentioned **The Banana Splits** cartoon/'live action' series from 1968-70... and yes, this kit could also double as one of the 'banana buggies'. ...So, if inclined, get your *Bingo*, *Fleagle*, *Drooper* and *Snorky* figures out of the loft, stock up with some psychedelic '60s' paints and then all you'll need... *are four more kits*!

Photoshop wizardary for the shots by Richard Farrell.

Kit purchased from Phil Howard of *Retro Models*.

Model built, constructed, painted and photographed by Chris Rogerson.

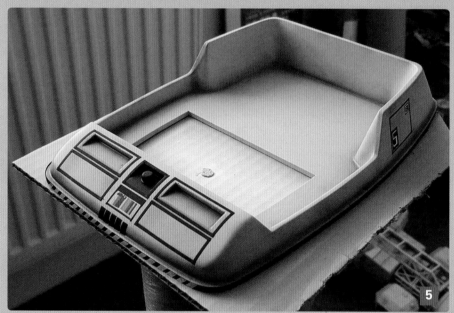

7

8

Space:1999's *Moon Buggy* is, of course, the six-wheeled, all-terrain land vehicle used by the *Alphans* on the Moon surface. It can carry two people and, as it is a rather small vehicle, it has a low transport capability in the space behind the seat. There is no steering wheel, but instead two handles, each operating one side of the *Buggy*, enabling it to be driven like a tank. The *Buggy* can operate both in vacuum and in the atmosphere of a planet and can be transported by *Eagles* (mainly as part of the regular reconnaissance mission pod equipment) to planets encountered on the Moon's journey.

The full size series' prop was based on the *Amphicat*, a real amphibious vehicle sold in North America at the time the show was filming. There were also studio models made in different sizes, from 3 to 46cm (the smallest being for background elements in diorama SFX shots, the largest example being remote controlled).

This *Comet* resin kit was given to me by a friend (he will recognise himself – a big thanks to him) to complete my **Space:1999** model collection. This is supposed to be a cast copied from a mould pulled directly from the 1:24th scale,

12cm long studio model. Underneath the body two pairs of holes are in evidence, which are certainly, in the case of the largest ones, the remnants of locations for the rods that connected to the rails that pulled the model during filming. The smaller holes seem to be for the steering handles (Or for electrical wires for pyrotechnic effects, perhaps?). If the kit really is a copy of the studio model, this is certainly not the case for the provided figure in spacesuit, that does not look at all like the astronauts from the *Revell 1:24th Gemini* kit that were originally used (the same figures that were also used in the *Command Module* of the 44" *Eagle* models).

The kit is roughly composed of seventeen resin parts: the body in two halves (top and bottom), two parts for the bench seat; headlights and side mirrors; six wheels, and the figure in three pieces (body and arms). There is very little surface detail, reflecting the look of the original miniature.

Refining Alpha's redoubtable runabout

Olivier Cabourdin
converts a 1/24 Moon Buggy kit

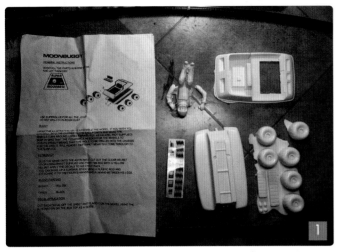

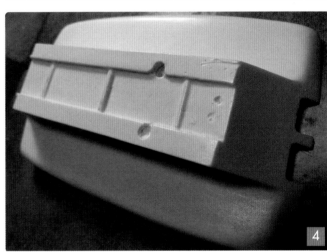

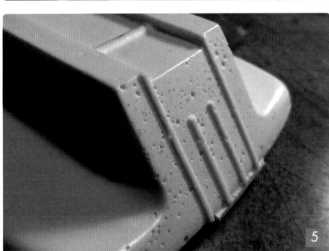

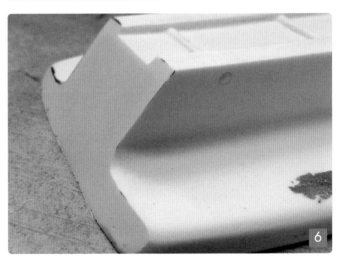

1: Contents of the kit.

2: The deteriorated paint of the original seat and backrest was cast as is.

3: The figure shows moulding shifts and significant gaps.

4: Underneath the *Buggy*, the pair of larger holes are remnants of locations for the rails rods that pulled the model during shooting stages. The tinier holes were certainly for the handles.

5: The rear side of the *Buggy* is full of bubbles.

6: The rear side sanded, clear of bubbles.

On the quality side the resin parts were full of air bubbles, there was a lack of resin in some areas, and there were gaps and mould misalignments. Hopefully, the simplicity of the subject meant it should be workable with not much difficulty. Curiously, the driving handles were not provided, nor metal axles to attach the wheels to the body. The supplied decal sheet was damaged and faded by time, so I did not use it.

I first built this kit in a hurry for an exhibit, leaving some work on it pending – so when Mike asked for an article on this subject, it was a good excuse to go back and finish it.

After a bath in hot soapy water, I started to work the upper and lower body parts. As they were slightly warped in the moulding, they were taken back to their correct shape by dipping them in boiling water then pressing them onto a flat surface (a table, for example). The rear side of the bottom part was completely full of air bubbles. Rather than trying to fill these, I chose the quicker method of sanding the surface with a belt and disc sander then adding a sheet of plastic card (of the sanded back width) to return to the correct level. Before sanding, I marked the edge with a pen to see how far in I was going. I ended up sanding 2mm back to get a clean surface without bubbles. After a dry test, I found that the step with the median lip (between the upper and lower body) looked visually rather better now, more to my taste, and that I did not need to add plastic sheet. So, in the end, this way to proceed proved to be even quicker than I initially thought! The edges were sanded to round their shape, and the raised stripes were then redone using 1mm x 0.75mm *Evergreen* strips.

The lack of material in the upper part of the body was filled with *Tamiya* bi-component filler. I don't use this often, and had forgotten how strong this stuff smells, so I let it harden in the garage for a whole day. Everything was then contoured again after a new run with the sander.

The dashboard of the kit did not satisfy me. The studio model seems to have been broken and quickly repaired on one corner, and the kit reflected this as it had been moulded as is. In the same way, the two raised panels were not straight. This is not a problem when the time on screen is brief, but is too ugly to come under sustained scrutiny as part of an exhibition model, so it was sanded flat, by hand this time, beginning with a heavy grade sandpaper and graduating to finer ones. The two rectangular panels were redone with 0.5mm width plastic card. In the

same way, I sanded smooth the seat and backrest that had a grainy surface, which, I realised later, might have come from the original parts themselves, with the paint having been damaged over the years.

To allow installation of the wheels, the underbody was carefully drilled from side to side to hold axles made from metal rod. I also prepared a plastic pipe of a diameter which allowed the axles to thread through, that would be cut to the correct lengths to align each side wheel on the same line once everything had been painted.

The side mirrors were added and the remaining defects on the body were then worked on (filling, sanding and so on). Before gluing the top and bottom together, the cabin was coated with primer, followed by white and then yellow paint, masked, and then the entire exterior covered with a heavy layer of spray putty. I expected this to reveal tons of new residual defects, but was surprised that there were only a few, allowing me to quickly glue the upper and lower parts of the body and fill the seam.

7: The strips are replaced on the *Buggy's* rear.
8: The upper and lower parts are glued together, secured with clamps while curing.
9: A last coat of spray primer to check everything.
10: Painting the black stripes all around the body necessitated a tedious masking stage.

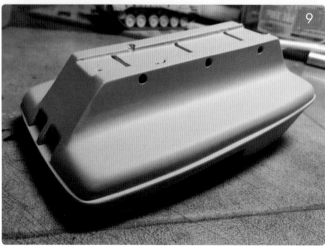

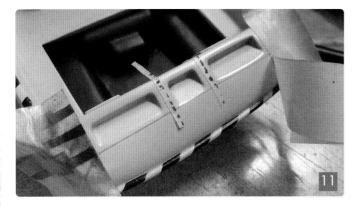

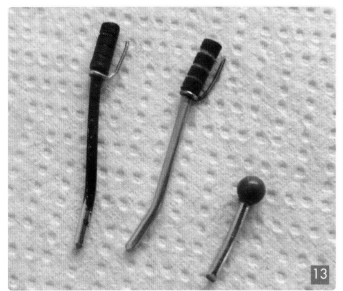

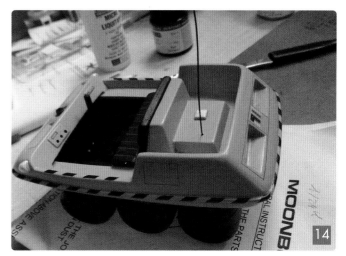

11: For the panels I used the same technique as done on the original model and drew them with a pencil. *Tamiya* tapes were used as guides.

12: The first attempt at the muffler in place. The wheel spacers are also noticeable.

13: Scratchbuilt handbrake and handles with their levers.

14: While still not finished, the *Moon Buggy* was ready for its first exhibit.

Following a last coat of primer, the *Buggy* received a base coat of *White* (*Citadel* spray can) and was then airbrushed with *Tamiya Matt Yellow* cut with a drop or two of orange to give it more punch. For colours like plain yellow, orange or, regularly, for red, a white base coat is needed to get a better finish. Once this was done I realised that I had erroneously painted the floor of the cabin yellow, as it should be black... which was fortunately easier to correct in this order than if I'd had to come back to yellow from black! A fastidious masking session was required to achieve the black stripes on the edge that runs all around the body. The *Buggy* then received a black wash to accentuate the shadows and break the bright yellow up a little.

At this stage of the build I found new reference images, showing the original vehicle on which the kit seems to have been moulded. It is clear that there is a muffler inside the right wheel mudguard,

a handle (certainly the handbrake) and two driving handles in the cabin, plus an antenna. Hatches and panels appear to have been drawn on with a pencil (as usual in Gerry Anderson productions).

For the muffler, I got my hand on a pen on which the button was made of chrome-plated brass, close to the required diameter. A corner was sanded to fit the curve of the mudguard, and two small holes drilled to set it easily into the body. For the panels, I chose the same technique as used on the original miniature, and drew them on with a pencil using masking tape as a guide. Each finished side was immediately gloss coated with *Future/Klear* to avoid fading or damage when working on the other sides.

After a light grey drybrush on the tyre treads, first painted black, the wheels, their axles and spacers were installed.

The provided headlights were fogged... even if this is accurate, I did not find them pretty. I therefore thermoformed new ones using clear plastic sheet from blister packaging. This was heated over a candle flame and pushed over the original part to shape it.

As stated earlier, I was in a hurry for an exhibit, so I only made one operating handle. Also the figure's feet did not allow for more, as whatever side he was positioned on, there was always one foot over one of the two locating holes. I therefore decided to come back to this, and to make a new handle, which could be in installed in its hole if the *Moon Buggy* was exhibited without the figure, or wedged between the astronaut's legs if he was in place. At this later date I also added the lever on the two handles using simple brass rod shaped with pliers, and made the handbrake with piano wire and a soft plastic ball cut from a joint knee part of a *Gundam* or *Macross* model kit.

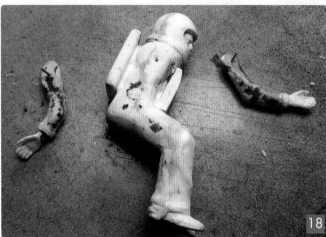

15: The new muffler, with its exhaust pipe.

16: The left arm of the figure looks like a *Playmobil* arm!

17: ...And after widening of the arm with putty...

18-19: With the application of different types of putties and fillers, it becomes difficult to see the remaining defects on the character, so he received a good layer of spray putty.

The antenna is made from a plastic wire label for clothing. This is flexible and strong, does not fear handling, and is easy to replace if needed. It was first painted black by error, and later corrected to white.

After the exhibit I found further new reference photos of the original studio model and realised my muffler was misplaced (that's why I'd had to sand an edge), it lacked the exhaust pipe (I suspected its existence, of course, but did not know where it was placed), my antenna was misplaced, and there were other errors (handles and handbrake) as detailed above. A new muffler was created with a large brass rod of the appropriate diameter, the exhaust pipe coming from my metal spare parts box.

Like the *Buggy*, the figure had its own moulding issues (shifts, gaps and bubbles) that were worked with *Tamiya* bi-component putty and car cellulosic filler, followed by a first rough sanding to see if there were any remaining defects. The right arm seemed to be attached not too badly to the body, but on the other side the left one looked skinny... like a *Playmobil* arm! It was subsequently enhanced with the addition of little fingers of *Tamiya* epoxy putty then shaped with a spatula. With the application of these different types of putties and fillers it became difficult to see any remaining defects on the figure, so he received a good layer of spray putty, finally showing only a few last tiny issues needing correction. To secure the arms to the body, small brass rods were added and the limbs were then set aside to be glued after painting.

I next focused on the figure's equipment. The back pack was not accurate, being too 'boxy' and looking as a single element when it should look more like two 'flattened bottles', so I rounded the edges and gave it a central groove. The front pack was left alone as its shape seems correct. For fun, and to complete his equipment, using 2mm width plastic card I scratchbuilt a mini *Stun Gun* and a *Comlock* in scale with the figure. The figure's helmet also lacked a visor and a fine strip going from the skull top and ending at the nape. The two were made by thermoforming plastic sheets (a clear one for the visor), heating them over a candle and pushing them against the helmet then allowing them to cool to the same shape. The outlines were then drawn onto the plastic and cut. The top strip was glued over the helmet, filled and primed.

After a final coat of primer, the character was ready for painting and received a base coat of *White* (*Citadel* spray can), then airbrushed with *Gunze Dark Orange*. The spacesuit creases were darkened with *Tamiya* red paint. He then received a very light black wash to shade

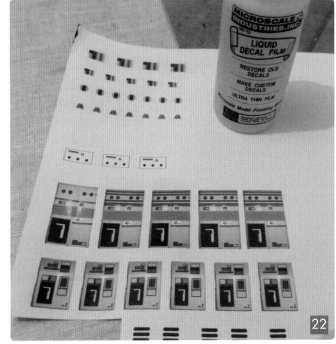

20: The *Alphan* with his scratchbuilt *Stun Gun* and *Comlock*.
21: The figure's visor is a clear plastic sheet thermoformed against the helmet to obtain the right shape.
22: The figure's back and front pack details panels printed on white paper, and protected with *Microscale* liquid decal film product.

any recesses or corners (helmet edges, glove cuffs...). The numerous belts of the spacesuit were then made using thin strips of a black tape found in a DIY shop.

As stated earlier, the decals provided with the kit were of poor quality: faded, and with printer banding clearly noticeable, so they were unusable. I drew new ones on my computer, using screen captures of the shows found on the web. After a few failed attempts to print on blank decal sheet (either white or transparent) with my inkjet printer, I was not able to get a correct result this time, so I came up with the solution of printing on white paper! To protect the ink, I generously coated the print with *Microscale* liquid decal film on each side. The paper is thicker than a decal would be, but at least I got a result.

As the finished model is rather small despite its 1:24th scale, I decided to made a lunar surface to highlight it when exhibited at conventions. The ground is a square taken from a foam plate shaped with a heat gun. The moon surface is a sandy paste made of a mixture of roughcast and glycero-based dark grey

paint, brushed over the shaped foam. Once it had fully cured (after one or two days), to create the dusty look of the lunar surface, I airbrushed on a light grey as horizontally as possible, and always in the same direction. This allowed each microscopic grain to be painted light grey on one side only, letting the other in its dark grey colour give the desired dusty result I wanted.

While the kit needed some work due to its quality issues, it ultimately proved to be a rather quick build, and I ended up with a result that I was, and still am, pleased with. It was also fun to build a kit copied directly from the model I watched with envy when I was a little boy in front of a black and white TV set.

This is a nice addition to the collection and a new part of my '*Child of Space: 1999*' project, started a few years ago with the *Launch Pad*, *Main Mission* and *Eagle Hangar* dioramas (see *21st Century Modeller Vol. 2*, still available from the publishers of this special).

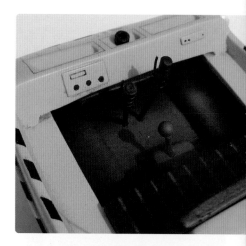

PRESERVING 1999

Super-collector James Winch has a mission in life: to track down and save as many original models and props from **Space: 1999** as he can. In the following pages Jim kindly shares with us a selection of images spotlighting some of the most treasured pieces in his collection.

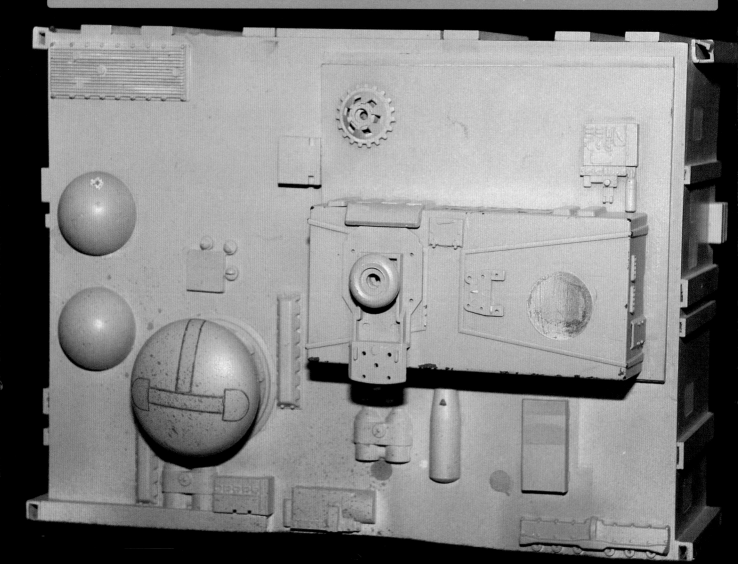

This spread: original *Alpha* building. This was repainted at some stage but the door and numbers are untouched. Size: 260mm wide, 190mm deep, 140mm high.

...As a child of the sixties, James Winch grew up on Gerry Anderson shows, and couldn't wait for the next episode or new series. Jim loved the puppet programmes, but when the live action shows started he was hooked...

'**UFO**, and then **Space: 1999**, were my life. I couldn't get enough of them. But as I grew older and real life took over the shows got pushed to the back of my mind.

'Then, one weekday on TV I saw that UK's *ITV 4* was showing **Space: 1999**, and my childhood came flooding back. In fact, it started my need to collect. My wife is totally to blame as to start me off she got me a *Konami Eagle* as a joke for my birthday. Little did she know! That was about eight years ago, and, boy, has my collection grown. I now have hundreds of models, be they *PE* or custom built or originals.'

Jim is always on the look out for new pieces and counts himself very lucky to own many original models.

Continued page 41...

Right: original medical signage.

Below (and bottom page 41): original stun gun – a background rather than a hero prop.

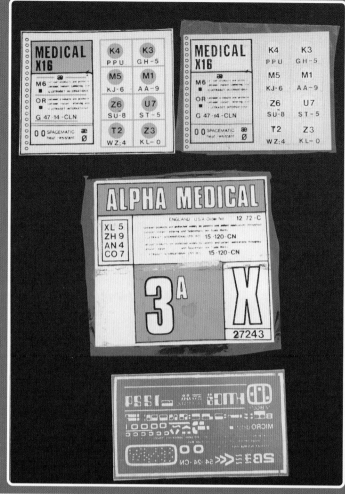

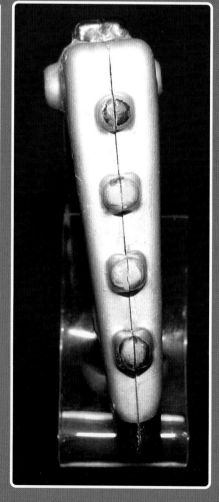

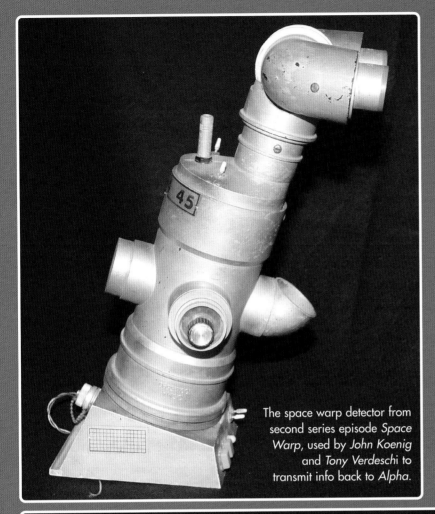

The space warp detector from second series episode *Space Warp*, used by *John Koenig* and *Tony Verdeschi* to transmit info back to *Alpha*.

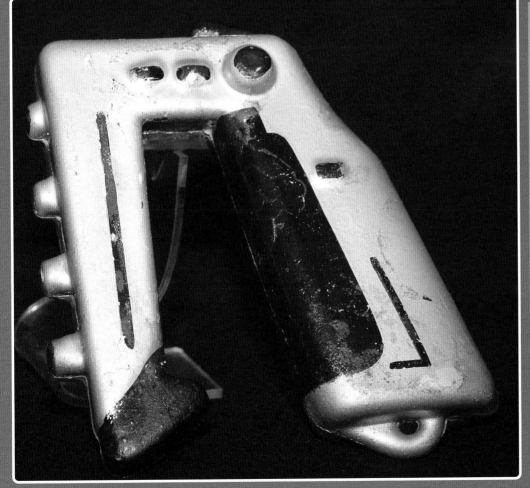

'My collection is growing all the time – in fact only in the last few weeks I have managed to get another derelict ship... you just never know! The joy that **Space** has given me is such that I now have friends all around the world, and I enjoy displaying my collection to the public, meeting old and new fans and chatting to kids and seeing the amazement on their faces.

'My goal, now that the **UFO** *Shado Jeep* I own is completed, is to restore *Moonbase Alpha* back onto a board with replacement launch pads and travel tubes.

'Watch this space. :-) '

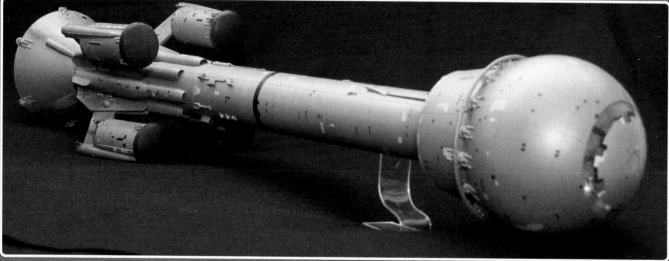

This page: original derelict ships from first season episode *Dragon's Domain*.
Blue ship is 900mm long by 230mm wide. Grey ship is 790mm long.

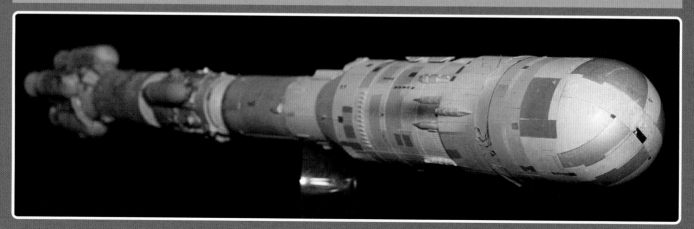

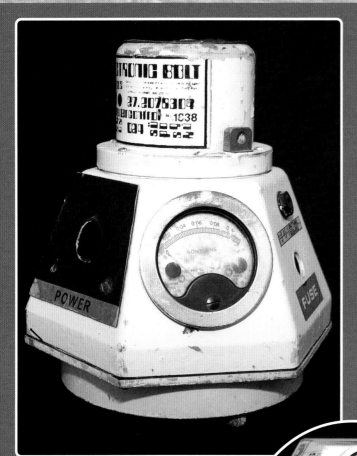

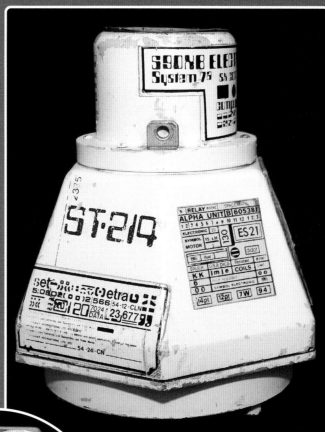

Radiation instrument from second season episode *All That Glisters*, as used by *Dave Reilly*. This prop also appears in other episodes. Size 230mm tall by 230mm wide.

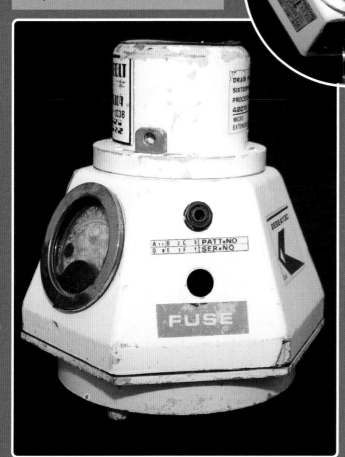

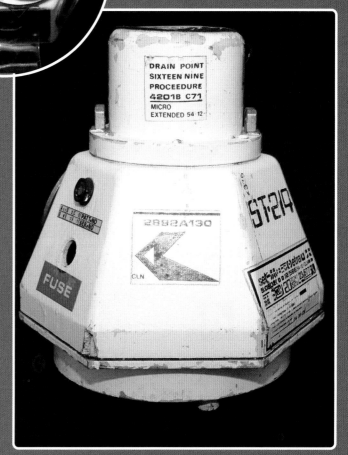

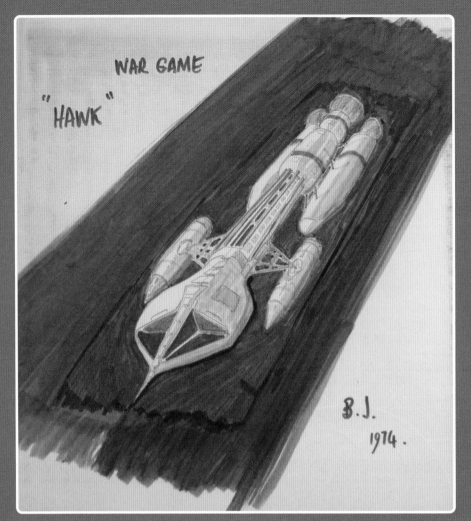

WAR GAME

"HAWK"

B.J.
1974.

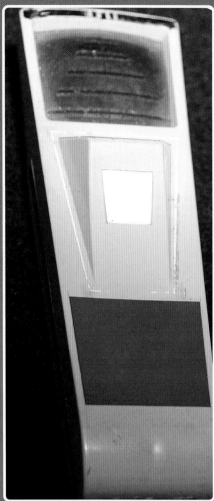

Top left: original design for the *Mark IX Hawk* by Brian Johnson from first season's *War Games*. Top right: *Lambda Factor* recorder from the same episode, used by *Sally Martin*. Above left: this is believed to be the original Buck to make the 22-inch *Eagle*. It has been changed as it wouldn't originally have had the cut-outs. On the back is newspaper print from the period. The little mask is from second season's *Devil's Planet* and featured on one of the building models.

Above: 'What can I say?' says Jim. 'The star model!'... Left: original storage box, as seen in many episodes. This has been repainted at some time, and the numbers have also been changed.

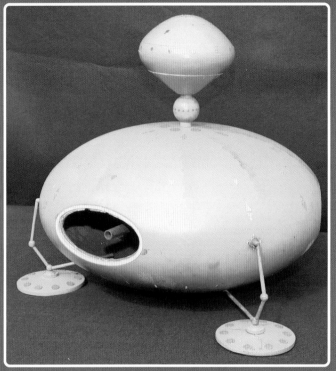

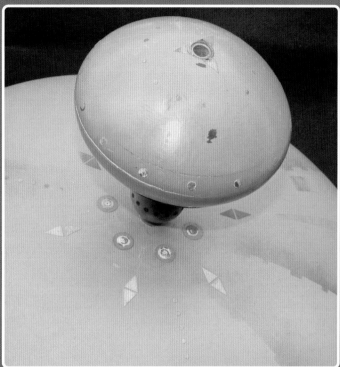

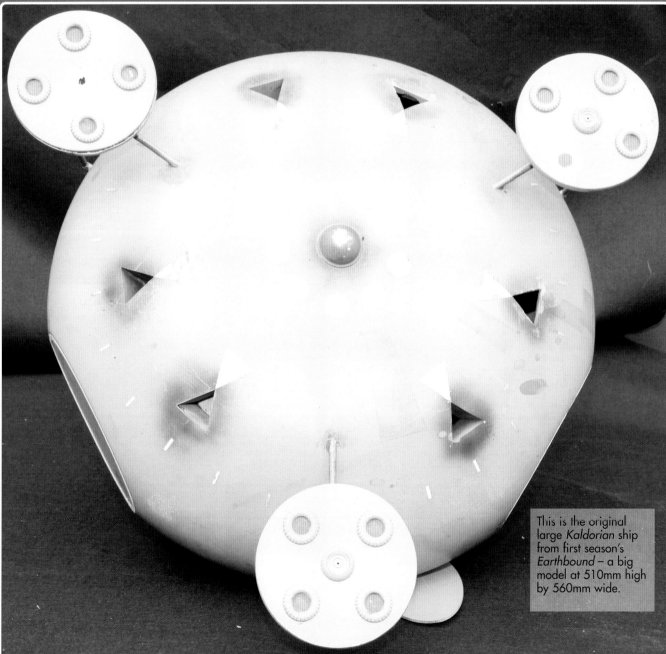

This is the original large *Kaldorian* ship from first season's *Earthbound* – a big model at 510mm high by 560mm wide.

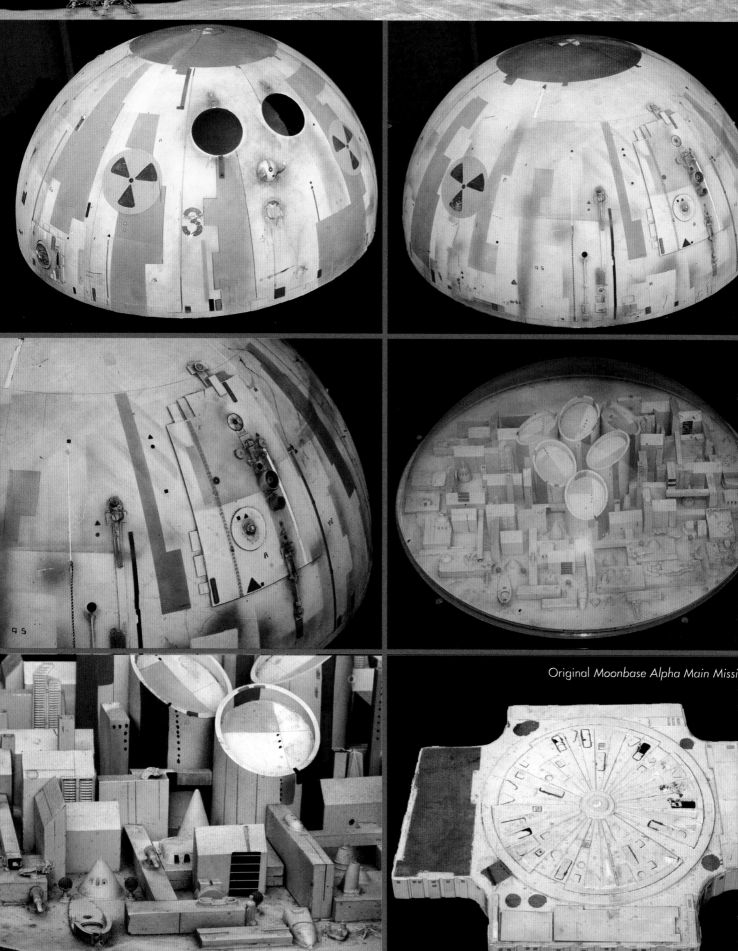

Original *Moonbase Alpha Main Missi*

Top: original *Nuclear Dome* from second season two-parter *Bringers of Wonder*.
Above: one of the original small domes from season two's *Journey to Where*. Jim owns seven domes in total.

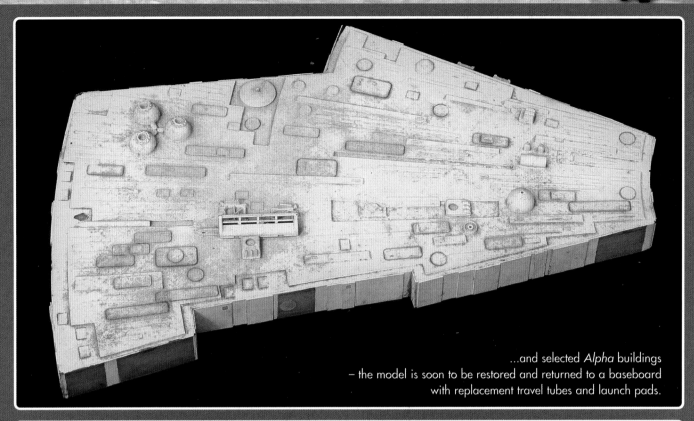

...and selected *Alpha* buildings
– the model is soon to be restored and returned to a baseboard
with replacement travel tubes and launch pads.

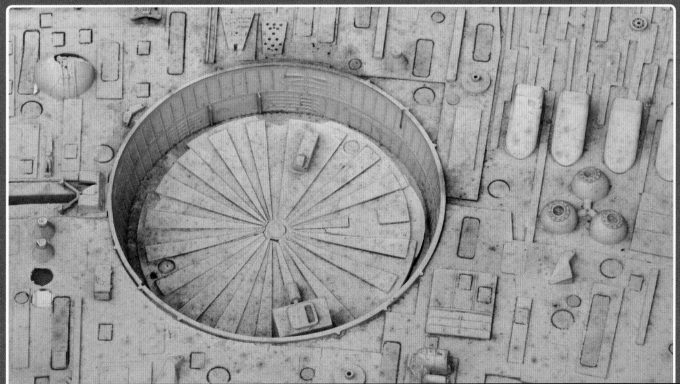

Original *Air Probes* from first season's *The Last Sunset*. The small one still has its hanging wire.

The orange model is a capsule from season two's *The Exiles*.

Left: *John Koenig's* original head gear from season two's *The Immunity Syndrome.*

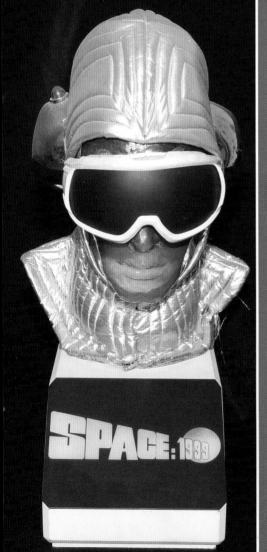

Original 44-inch *Eagle Cargo Pod.*

Opposite top right and above: the *Golos Tower* model from season two episode *The Exiles*. Size: 585mm high by 450mm wide. Below: this final picture shows just a section of Jim's display room at home… 'This is a small part of my collection – I would need to move out to display it all!'

The *Swift* was an Earth ship that disappeared without trace on a discovery mission with other sister ships, and which was used to menace the *Alphans* during their journey in the season two episode *Brian the Brain*. Its design fits in perfectly with the earth style established in the series, and is inspired by the *Eagle*, with its elongated shape and insect like cockpit ('beak'). It is also recognisable by its two large spinal dorsal tanks.

This multimedia kit, produced and designed by Alexandre Dumas/*Sci-High Models*, is a must have for any **Space: 1999** modeller. Alex kept me in touch with progress of during the months of its making, and I was lucky enough to receive one of the first copies. It is in scale with 11" *Eagles* – both the old *Airfix/Fundimensions/ERTL* examples and now the *Round 2* kit – and also with the *Product Enterprise* diecasts (now long out of production), making her 36cm long once finished. The kit consists of around one hundred resin parts, fifteen metal and plastic rods and wires, and, if you choose the Deluxe kit, turned aluminium bells instead of resin ones.

Comparison with pictures of the original studio model reveals the proportions are there. I was unable to find an error and all details have been accurately replicated. The casting of the resin parts is clean, the landing gear shock absorber parts even being hollowed out into a tube! The few air bubbles found were mainly located under the neck (though more would be revealed later). There is also a decal sheet for the tiny maintenance markings and hash strips. Windshields, antiglare panels, and two orange and red decal sheets were also provided, but I would set these aside and use paints instead.

Of the many metal rods and tubes included, the majority would go to form the landing gear and legs (through complex bending with pliers), with some acting as strengthening struts between some of the heavier parts (body, command module, main engine and main bell).

The turned metal bells are absolutely superb – clean, without any defect and, last but not least, very accurate. The large bell has grooves that perfectly match the original studio model counterpart. These bells would make a big difference to the final model.

I first received the kit without instructions (unfinished at the time) and,

Lost In Space

Olivier Cabourdin
finds the disappearing Swift
Earth ship a challenging build.

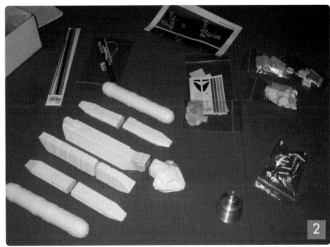

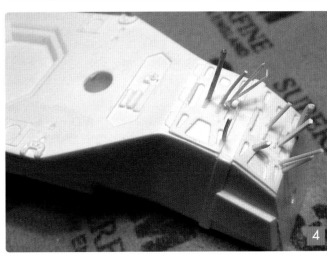

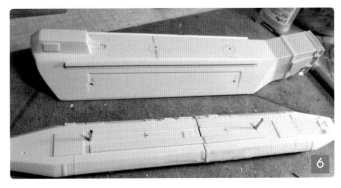

01: Kit box art.
02: Contents of the kit.
03: There were very few moulding seams to work.
04: Filling bubbles under the neck.
05: The alignment of the side, upper and central pods was secured using clamps on a wood plank or on the workbench table while the glue was curing.
06: Metal rods and holes are prepared during assembly to, after the painting stage, facilitate the positioning and strengthen the gluing.

given the number of parts, I have to say that without them placement of many of the smaller parts did not come together and some remained totally obscure to me. Once the instructions were received, it all became clearer, of course. They are well done... explicit for a regular modeller, but also for a less experienced one, with many photos taken during assembly of the test shot that speak louder than text. Many

helpful tips are also offered. However, assembly is complex and delicate (particularly the leg construction step), so this kit is intended for the experienced modeller.

For the record, instruction measurements were in the imperial system, so calculating conversions were easy... on the other hand, finding appropriate drill bits in

the birth country of the metric system proved to be too difficult, so I had to use close but not exact ones.

After a bath in soapy water where the parts were brushed to remove demoulding residue (an essential step with resin kits), I started to sand the moulding seams. This could have been tricky on the two long upper tanks (it's often difficult to sand cylindrical or spherical parts as their curvature usually suffers) but ultimately there was rather a lot of excess material needing to be removed so the process went both well and quickly.

The next step was to fill any bubbles with small plastic rods and superglue, which is a less time consuming method than trying to fill them with putty. Bubbles were not numerous on this kit, and were mainly located on the small discs of the feet (the toes) and under the neck of the central module (where the detail is based on a *Leopold german railway gun* model kit part).

There were also some on the beak, behind the cheeks, that proved to be the most difficult to remedy, as these were tiny, located just below the surface, and concentrated near a moulding seam. I didn't notice them on the first side, and this type of bubble is extremely difficult to eliminate, as sanding filled bubbles reveals

new ones. I used a much softer approach when sanding the other side, and was able to avoid a second headache.

I started assembly of the sides and upper pod, which are glued end to end, strengthening the bonding with metal rods, using slow curing superglue, guides and clamps to secure the alignment. The putty applied on the seam was cleaned with acetone (nail varnish remover). Curiously this slightly damaged the surface of the resin (the first time this has happened for me). I tried to make this good, but was not satisfied, so I set the assembly aside to address later following a good shot of primer (later proving to be sufficient). The instructions suggested I now glue the side modules to the central body, but I did not follow them in order to be able to paint these parts separately and more easily. Metal rods are provided to secure the modules to the central body, holes being made at appropriate locations, but, like the modules, these would be

glued after painting. The hinges of the legs were glued following the useful method explained in the instructions, using a rod as a guide.

The command module ('*Beak*' or '*Head*') would also be secured to the central body through the neck with a metal rod, so holes were prepared and drilled. The same method was used to connect the main bell to the rear engine and main body, the toes to the feet, the three rear engine pods to the main engine, etc. The fuel pipes connecting these secondary engines to the main body gave me a hard time because I had initially wrongly measured their locations and angles.

The dorsal tanks, containing freon gas for the engines on the original studio model, are joined together by two small plates of resin moulded directly with a brass rod going through for support. It is intended that these two plates are then glued onto the top pod, but I found this too

07: The brass tube holding out the main bell and engines against the central body.
08: First failed attempt to keep the dorsal tank plates removable with plastic wedge and brass rods.
09: Two tiny brass rods added to hold the upper tank bells, without glue so the bells remain removable for transporting the model.
10: A wood stand is screwed to the main body to hold it at the right height to help while making the legs.

fragile, so needed to find a way to create a better, secure system. The trouble was the plate thickness was not adequate to accept small vertical rods as on the side modules, so I tried to create additional strength with plastic strip where the plate meets the top pod grooves. I was then able to add tiny brass rods, but we will see later that this proved to not be enough. On the back of the tanks it is also better to secure the two small nozzles with thin brass, and even keep them unglued for easier transport and storage.

Having avoided this next step for as long as I possibly could, I finally had to tackle the dreaded legs. This is by far the most complicated stage of this kit. They consist of several rods needing to be bent in all directions, metal pipes to cut and fit together, and resin parts to plant on. The *Swift* is a long-legged ship. The legs could not be made of resin (too fragile), and the result would have been, I think, unsatisfactory with cast metal. In short, the

right solution was chosen, but is a real challenge to assemble... Fortunately the instructions were really useful, offering tips, such as using a wood stand screwed to the central body to hold it at the proper height. So, with a clever set of pliers, drill, sore fingers and swear words, and re-gluing of parts coming apart (under a new rain of swear swords), I ended up with legs that suited me. It was also important to remember to add the needed plastic tubes and shock absorber resin parts after each folding step, otherwise their inclusion was not possible, with going back and unfolding the rod the only way to proceed.

The hardest stage over, it remained to add their strut braces, made of brass rod and plastic tube. For their length, it is better to directly measure this on the dry build legs rather than stay with the instruction measurements, as there may be some tiny differences between legs... here, an error of 2mm does not forgive! In this kit these struts are only details, as the legs

clearly have sufficient strength to support the weight without any strengthening. I therefore kept them separate to instal after painting. The detailing of the shock absorbers is accomplished with a provided grey tape, which I replaced with masking tapes (*Tamyia*, *Micron*) that I realised were to the proper width, thus saving me time on cutting!

I took care with the VTOL engines to avoid a conflict with the legs, as they are really near to each other. As they attach to the side modules, the angle of the rods needed care when drilling locating holes as these differ from front to back.

The *Swift* then joined a long queue of kits awaiting paint... but with a priority pass. A first coat of primer revealed rows of micro bubbles on the side pods, quickly eliminated with putty.

Space: 1999's earth ship base colour is not pure white but slightly off-white, so I

11: The main column legs prior to folding. 12: The main column legs folded.
13: The hardiest step was folding the brass leg struts, without damaging the plastic tubes and shock absorbers that needed
    to be added at each step of the folding process.
14: Detailing the shock absorbers with *Tamiya* masking tape.

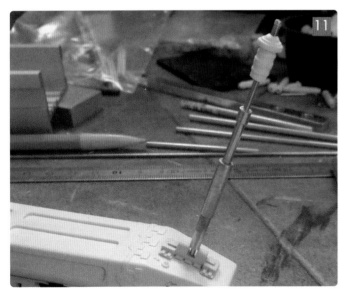

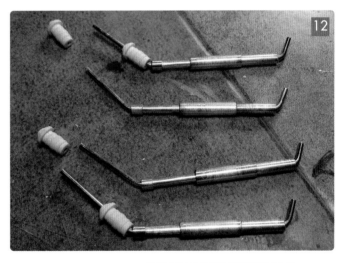

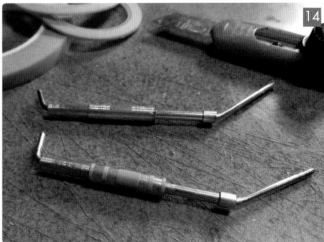

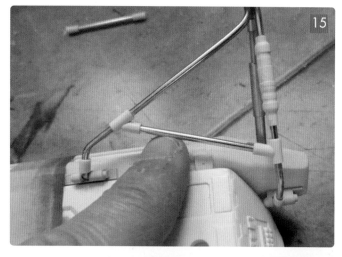

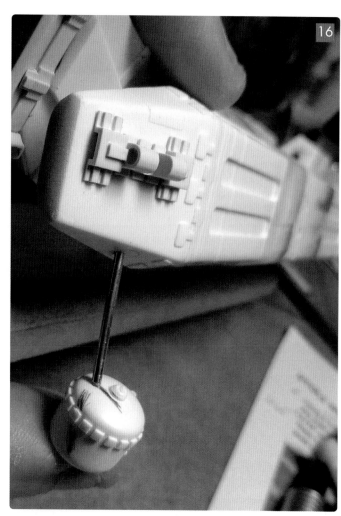

15: The strut braces were prepared, cut and sanded to the correct length and angles, and kept apart to be glued after painting.

16: Drilling holes for the holding rod of the side VTOL engines was also tricky. Despite the pencil marks, it was finally mainly done by eye and freehand.

17: The base colour is an off-white (*Matt White* with few drops of *Sky Grey*).

mixed *Flat White* with *Sky Grey* (*Tamiya XF-19*). Over a white background you can easily see the difference. Over a more colourful or black background, the eye and camera views it as white (the intended goal). All parts were sprayed, as white is also a needed base to obtain nice red, yellow or orange colours, and the doors were painted in a light grey.

Now came the difficulty of finding the correct red colour, which is, in fact, not a full red on the studio model. I even interpreted it as orange on some references, with a heavily worked panelling made of different levels of orange to red. The white panels were therefore masked, and a basic orange (*Tamiya X-6*) was airbrushed.

The panelling was then carried out following photos of the studio model to make the end result as accurate as I could. It was achieved with red paint, but staying subtle and playing with the flow of the airbrush to softly darken the orange base

colour. I used a heavily thinned paint (around an 80/20 thinner/paint ratio) and very low pressure 0.3 - 0.4 bars (5psi, I think, very near the loss of pressure), with the airbrush in double action (to achieve softness in the paint flow rate). This way, painting a panel required several passes to thoroughly paint it. I played with this to add more or less red paint over the orange, achieving lots of tones of colours, from orange to red-orange to near full-red panels.

The windshield and antiglare panels were finished in black (using the decals as a template). Light beige panels were added here and there and the remaining strips on the dorsal were painted with a mixture of light orange and light pink. The red, orange and blacks stripes on the *Command Module* and the legs were done with the airbrush.

The last stage of panelling consisted of creating shades on the 'white' and 'orange' areas in different tones of grey, again using only one grey (*Neutral Grey XF-53*) and

playing with the airbrush. Black streaks near gauges and nozzles were done with poorly thinned black in the airbrush to create a spotty effect.

The ends and insides of the bells were weathered with *Alclad Jet Exhaust* and matt black. The tiny nozzles of the dorsal tanks are resin parts, so I painted these with a base of *Alclad Jet Exhaust*, followed by *Steel* and *Chrome* to bring them closer to their aluminium sisters. Sadly, I realised that I had forgotten to mask the shock absorber aluminium pipes on the landing gear, so they were painted white. Rather than trying to scrape the paint for an uncertain result, I preferred to airbrush these areas with *Alclad Chrome*.

The painting stage over, I applied a gloss coat of *Johnson's Future/Klear* in readiness for washes and decals. The black wash is very light here because the goal was not to dirty the ship, but rather to highlight the details. There were a bunch of decals that

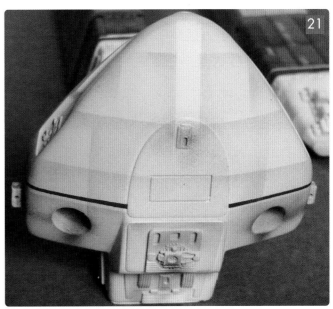

18: The white is also a perfect base to airbrush with yellow or, as here, orange.
19: The first panelling effect is done with full red, playing with the flow of the airbrush.
20, 21 & 22: The second panelling is done in the same way, this time using neutral grey.

needed to be cut from the sheet which were quite fragile, and many would lose a little colour in the process. As I damaged one of the large red striped decal strips that circle the dorsal tanks, I had to hand paint the damaged area. To hide the difference I created a small black area of weathering with the airbrush to simulate a dirt panel.

To seal everything I needed a satin coat before final assembly. This time I wanted to test *Microscale Micro Satin* (thinned with water), and, as I could not see any difference after drying, I next selected *Micro Flat* ...with no better result. I therefore went back to *Prince August Air Matt*, strongly mixed with *Tamiya* thinner (proportions around 10/90) without alcohol, to prevent white halo marks.

As with previous steps, the final assembly brought its own troubles. Firstly, curiously the legs no longer had the same tilt as initially. So disassembly, correction with pliers and reassembly was needed. Several

small parts were broken and/or bent during these manipulations. I repaired as best I could, then repainted the offending areas to mask this. Fortunately, the damage was in areas that were somewhat hidden. Secondly, the same thing occurred with the engine pod fuel pipes that no longer connected to the main body. I won't detail everything, but I had to get out the airbrush

a few more times to correct two or three more assembly gaffs... under another flow of well-chosen swear words! The method of holding the dorsal tank support plates did not work, these being still too slim, so I had to go back to a more conventional but reliable method: *screws*! The final step in completing the model was to install the wires running to the VTOL.

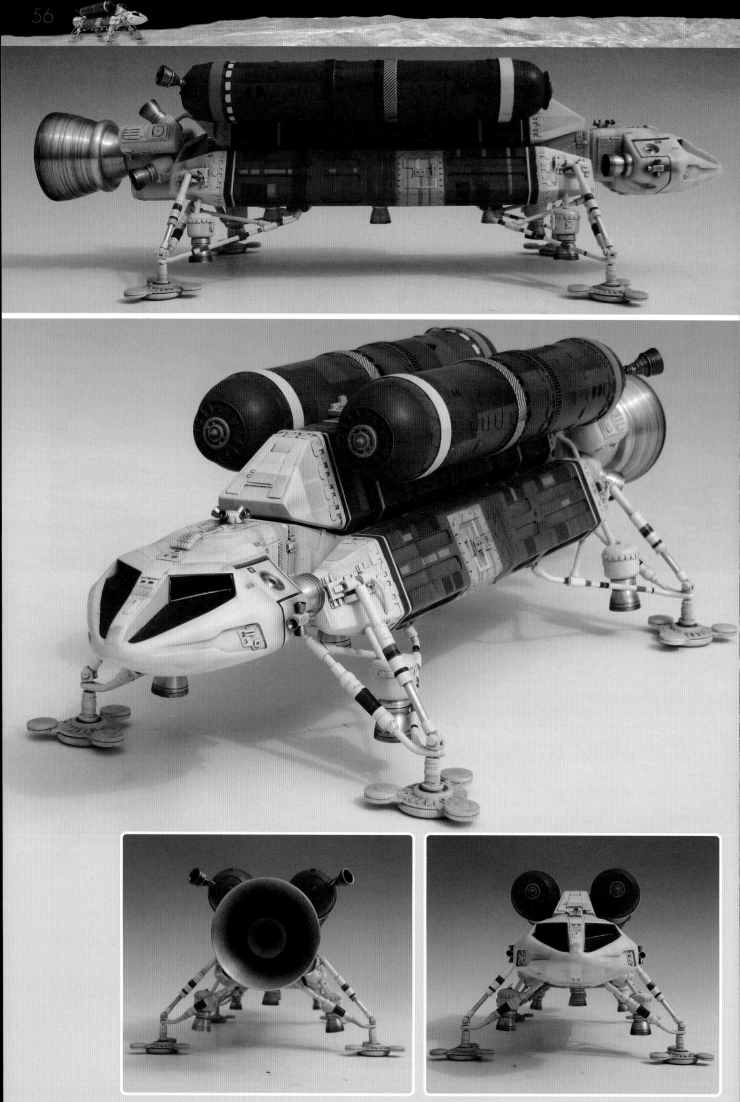

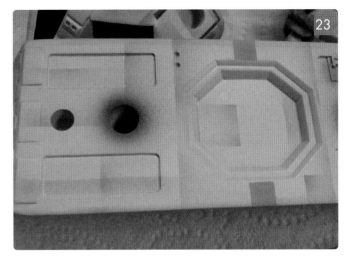

23: Black streaks are done with a poorly thinned black in the airbrush.

24: The *Swift* before installation of the dorsal tanks and sitting between two *Product Enterprise Eagles*. It is a bigger ship than the *Eagle*.

25: In the end, the dorsal tank plates are screwed to the upper module.

Despite the difficulty of assembly, the result is a crisp and superb model of the *Swift*. And I have to say that, despite the few troubles I met and the effort needed, I had a lot of fun building it, especially when painting the panelling, which differs significantly from the all-white or all-grey spaceships we usually see. And I'm quite proud of the final result. It was finished just in time for its first exhibition at a convention in Paris, where the theme of our stand was, of course, **Space: 1999**.

...Hey, Alexandre... we need a *Superswift* now!

Return of the Infernal Machine

Theo P. Stefanski revisits and recreates an iconic Space: 1999 guest craft

In a moment of delusion, when I thought I had free time between projects, I hit upon the idea of producing a guest ship kit (photo 1) from **Space: 1999**. Of course, I didn't pick a simple one, like the ship from the Christopher Lee episode *Earthbound...* I decided on *Gwent* from *The Infernal Machine*. It reminded me somewhat of the space crawler from *Mattel's Major Matt Mason* and the overall look of *Gwent* is intriguing as well as menacing.

So, carried forward by this wild idea, I began with some basic drawings. Two *Gwent* models were used in filming, a large and a smaller version. The original big *Gwent* model was allegedly destroyed by Nick Allder at the end of shooting. I knew of only one photograph of this

original model, so most of the drawings were based on Blu-ray freeze frames, and, with this scant information, I began to build patterns based upon the big *Gwent* model, which has the majority of screen time.

I originally wanted to create a form out of wood, but as I was pressed for time, I resorted to what was at hand: black styrene and drain pipe (photo 2), the latter dictating the overall size. I then built up panels for the main body, adding and subtracting material until I had a shape I was satisfied with. The forward area was built hollow – this way someone with time on their hands could possibly motorise it with a small gear box, perhaps from the *Tamiya* WWI British tank. However, no provision or parts will be offered in the kit

for this madness, and I may delete this feature in the future.

The contours of the main body feature a central wide spine at the front, on which sits the glass dome. This was not as simple as it sounds, or looks, on the smaller model *Gwent*. After closer examination of many additional freeze frames, the spine appeared to be shallower in the centre, before increasing in thickness towards the front, culminating in a sort of chin under the dome, before ending in a long curve underneath. It took considerable rounds of sanding – filling – sanding to accomplish this look, and quite a lot of work for a guest ship on a TV show. Small half round strips were added for the under-the-chin area (photo 3). I could not detect any recognisable kit parts on the

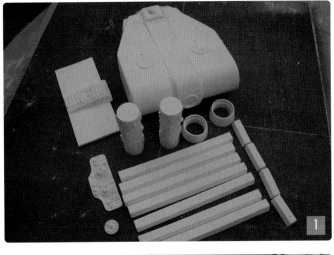

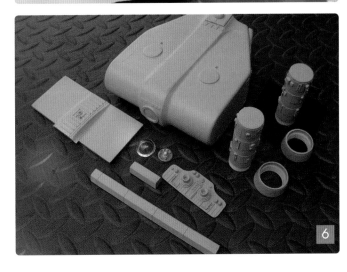

model from the Blu-ray frames, nor could I get any in this scale, so I approximated with card and very small parts. Having said this, upon a closer look, at the back end it appeared that two ship/airplane hull halves were attached. To recreate these, I formed and shaped built-up styrene. Underneath the tail there is a large half sphere which operates as a landing skid when on the lunar surface. As there is no direct shot of this area, I built up a radial block-like pattern of card (photo 4). I added to the back plate of the body two main nozzles plus some bits, including

some modern *Eagle* parts. I created some light panel lines, although for this era they would have mostly drawn them on. The main body was sprayed up in *Mr. Surfacer* and wet sanded it to a smooth finish. The circle inside the dome is from a 1/32nd scale *Heinkel III* with some additional bits. The clear dome came from a commercially available source, so that saved me the trouble of casting it myself.

Next, on to those dreaded paddle wheels. The main body's dimensions make the hubs one inch in diameter but,

strangely, I could not source styrene, *Plexiglas* or *ABS* in that size in this country (USA). I must remember to stay metric next time. I settled for Butyrate, which is not my favourite material. Thin bands were glued on and details, which appeared quite crude in my still frames, were found or approximated. The collars these fit into were made of the same material on my drill press/lathe. I first made a test run of one of the 32 foot pads. I built up this first pad using styrene once again. The undersides of the pads are slightly rounded but not a full curve. Each

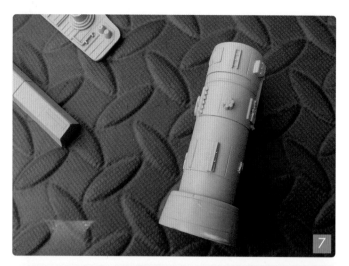

wheel consists of four groups of four paddles/feet. The spokes on either end oppose each other and the two middle rows are a transition from one to the other. For production kits I plan to have a jig made to pre-drill the holes for each brass spoke. Otherwise, the builder would be left to fend for themselves on this matter.

With all patterns completed (photos 6-8) it was time to make the moulds. For economy's sake, wood boxes were constructed. The main body was screwed to one wall, which would be its filling point when casting. It is also the only two-part mould for this kit. I used a rubber called *GI 100* for the mould. It captures detail very well... sometimes too well. Surprisingly, the first pour produced a usable cast. The other parts followed suit. The feet of the wheel were produced as sticks, which needed to be cut into four pieces, and eight will be provided in the kit.

For this build, I plotted out each of the holes for the hub spokes and drilled them by hand. The spokes appear not so much as a spiral, but an angled line. The spokes are brass, cut at 45mm made from 1/16th rod, and the feet are spaced 38mm from the hub, using a scrap plastic gauge.

With all parts except the dome in place it was sprayed up in *Tamiya* primer (photo 10). Next up was a coat of *Tamiya Gun Metal*, which was a little too dark, but an overall mist would fix that later. The panel work was next, using different darker metallic *Humbrol Greys*, starting with number 53, then tinted with *Blue* on the front. The base of the hubs was done in *Yellow*, as were some details. On the stills, there are round yellow circles on the feet, on one side only, but not in all shots, so I decided to omit those. The two wheel assemblies fit onto the main hull with a tight fit, but could be removed if needed. There is a stripe pattern on the front face of the hull, but since I was unable to generate decals at this point (photo 9), I used a stripe set made by *Microscale*. I utilised black, yellow and silver sets, sealed with *Walthers Solvaset*. The whole machine was sealed in a combination of semi-gloss and flat. Lastly, the dome was glued to a very thin sheet of black plastic and trimmed to prevent seeing the bare resin of the hull. Finally complete, it would go before the camera as pictured here. I now, finally, have a kit of one of the best guest ship/machines of any SF show, even though I had to make it myself. ...Now, on to produce production batches – and just maybe build a motorised one for myself, so I might on occasion fly it around the house whilst doing a Leo McKern voice impression.

Theo P. Stefanski can be contacted at:
ZeroGModels@yahoo.com

The one that got away

Olivier Cabourdin models Small Art Works' Ultra Probe beak

The *Ultra Probe* appeared in one of the best (if not *the* best) episode of **Space: 1999**, *Dragon's Domain*, in season one. This was a long range ship with a crew of four on a scientific deep space mission to explore the newly discovered planet *Ultra*. Something terrible happened when the expedition reached its destination, with *Tony Cellini*, the pilot of the probe ship, managing to escape using the *Command Module* as a life boat, and returning to earth alone following a six-month journey through space.

The subject of this article is James Small's resin kit of the front module of the *Ultra Probe*, also known as the *Command Module*, or *Beak*. The kit is in scale with the *Eagle* kits from *Airfix* and *Warp* and also with *Product Enterprise*'s 12-inch diecast model, and offers eighteen parts, plus instructions and a decal sheet. The resin parts are nicely and cleanly cast, without any air bubbles, and the accuracy seems very good when compared to the bigger and more detailed studio model... I could not, in fact, identify any corrections that needed to be made. Three different models of the probe were built for the episode, respectively in scale with the 12", 22" and 44" *Eagle* models, the smallest

being very crude and the largest highly detailed to allow for closer shots.

With such quality, assembly of the kit was mostly straightforward, requiring little more than some quick sanding along the seams. However, the clamp arms that secured the *Command Module* to the main body of the probe ship were very fragile, and one broke while I was sanding it. The four shoulder covers also needed a little sanding to their inside faces to allow the arm articulation parts to sit within them correctly and facilitate articulation of the arms themselves.

Sanding the engine bell seams was also a quick and simple task, although at this stage I realised that the two small bells on the back of the ship were missing from the kit, so these were quickly replaced by bell parts from a *Kotobukyia* upgrade set.

I wished to display the model on a stand but did not want to have any apparent holes on the model. I therefore drilled into the two tiny rear engine bells so two metal rods could be plugged into these from my display stand. In this way, the model shows no holes when unplugged from its stand. One day I intend to complete the

Ultra Probe ship, and these same holes will then be used to attach the *Command Module* to the body of the ship.

As with my other **Space: 1999** subjects, I chose an off-white as the base colour (a mix of white plus a few drops of *Tamiya Sky Gray*). The bells were airbrushed with *Alclad* paint followed by a darker colour at the edge. The decal sheet quality left much to be desired and was the worst aspect of this kit, with colours not being sharp enough. I therefore elected not to use them, with the exception of the *Ultra Probe* insignia that feature on each side of the nose.

The panels were painted on *twice*... The first time I did not attempt to be accurate with their size and location and airbrushed some random light grey panels on to have something interesting to break up the all-white surface. Then the red, black and grey stripes were applied, following the configuration seen on the biggest studio model. I wanted only a subtle weathering, achieved via a light black wash.

The model then made its way to a few exhibitions with the rest of my **Space:**

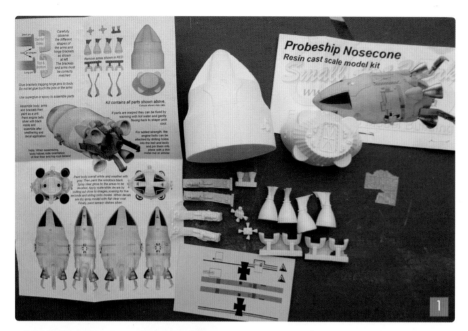

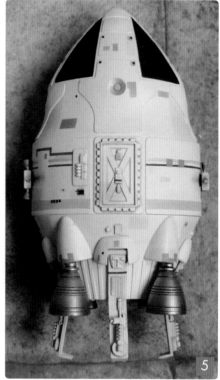

1: Contents of the resin kit.
2: Off-white base colour applied.
3–4: First livery applied with inaccurate panels and a basic display stand.
5–6: Modified livery, more accurate to the bigger studio model.
7–8: The new stand made from plexiglass and featuring a Moon print.

1999 collection... managing to lose 4 RCS bells during its travels. Also, with time, I found I was not satisfied with my initial paint job, finding it too simple. I therefore made a few modifications...

First, I had to find new RCS bells to replace the missing ones, and discovered some close matches in the spares box. To enhance the paintwork I began by airbrushing the base colour over most of the already applied light grey panels. Following reference photos, I then created

new, tinier and more accurate panels with light and medium greys, using tiny mask stencils made from plastic sheet. The weathering was kept light, and was completed by adding smoke streaks from the side RCS thrusters. I also added the hoses that connect the body to the arms using thin electrical wires. Creating a more accurate look, these also help the arms to stay in place.

I was not satisfied with my first display stand – made quickly from a CD pack box and two metal rods bent to lead from the box to the holes in the rear bells. I therefore imagined something more sophisticated: two metal rods now come down from the back bells and plug into a

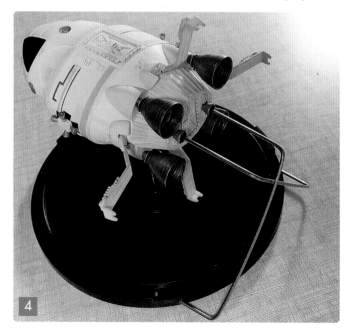

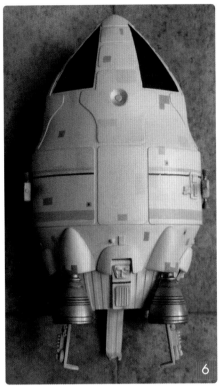

4mm wide plexiglass strip, shaped into a 'U' with a heat gun, itself plugged into a wooden disk. The disk is hidden by a print of the Moon, backed with black drawing paper to eliminate any transparency issues.

This was a rather quick build of a very nice little resin kit, that later became the first model of my 'Child of Space:1999' project (see the publishers' *21st Century Modeller, Vol. 2*). Looking at it now, I think it needs further modification... the rest of the probe ship, perhaps... or a larger, studio scale brother!

Alpha spacesuits – the inside story

David Sisson painstakingly restores a classic piece of Space:1999 costuming

When I watch a science fiction film or television series my main interest is in the models and special effects but I also enjoy looking at the sets and costumes, especially the spacesuits. In fact my respect for any production is often affected quite a lot by the quality of the spacesuits – or lack of them, as many television shows over the years have often not bothered to feature them. This could be for reasons such as trying to save money, problems with actors wearing them, and the possibility that they might look really bad! This is a shame because I find it very difficult to take any space related show seriously if the actors just walk around in their normal outfits in very dangerous environments.

My favourite spacesuits are from the Gerry Anderson television shows **Space: 1999** and **UFO** (the latter being made originally for his feature film **Doppelganger**), and the classic **2001: a space odyssey**. I almost bought a **Space: 1999** suit at an auction during a *Fanderson* convention in the early 1990s but it went for a tremendous amount of money, which I believe was £180! How times, and prices, have changed. Every time I thought about missing out on this purchase I would bash my head against a wall and curse my stupidity, but luckily for me in the early 1990s collector Phil Rae bought the entire Gerry Anderson props collection from *Alton Towers* (UK) and had a spare spacesuit for sale. Nine

years of regret meant that I wasn't letting this one slip by and so it was something that I just had to buy regardless of cost.

There were at least six complete spacesuits made for the television series, and possibly a couple more basic fabric suits. The costume I bought is marked as 'Suit 4', which is a little bit on the small side and only just fits me, together with the 'Suit 1' rubber neck collar assigned to Martin Landau. Whenever I watch the series I always try to see if my suit is being used and who is wearing it, which is pretty difficult to do even watching HD Blu-ray discs. I am helped by the fact that all the suits seem to have small differences – mine being one of two that have a white zip on

Top—left to right: 1999 convention. Suit 3 – Mark Shaw, Suit 4 – David Sisson, Suit 6 – Andrew Frampton, Zienia Merton suit – Jim Winch.

Preparing to assemble.

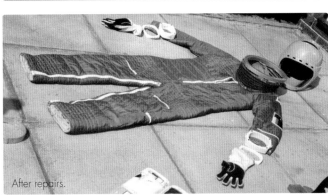

After repairs.

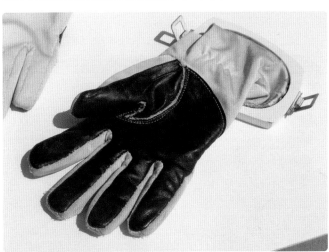

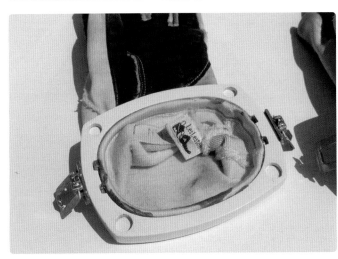

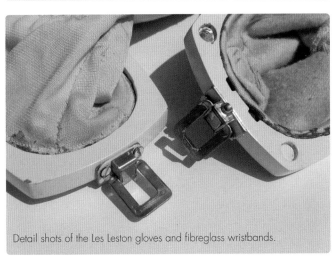

Detail shots of the Les Leston gloves and fibreglass wristbands.

the left arm. Often it seems to be worn by a minor character but I have definitely seen Barry Morse wearing it, and also, I believe, Prentice Hancock and Catherine Schell.

Unfortunately the suit had been used in a public display at both Blackpool (UK) and *Alton Towers* for a long time, and apparently owned and looked after by people who didn't appear to have any great interest in it. As a result it was not in a very good condition – in fact, like most of the original studio items I have

managed to acquire over the years, it looked completely knackered! For my money I got a one-piece orange bodysuit, a pair of connecting gloves, a rubber neckpiece and a helmet. I also got an old mannequin that had been assembled and fixed in a pose whilst it was wearing the suit, and as a result I had to drive home with this large figure wedged in the car, then drag it into the garage where I could smash it up using a very large hammer before I could then remove the costume.

Once I got the suit off the dummy I examined it closely, but not too closely because it hadn't been cleaned for around 15 years and my skin was crawling from just being near it! The single-piece suit was nearly in three pieces as the right arm was coming off at the shoulder and there was a split down the back – luckily both were due to the seams giving way and not the material. The material in question is a bright orange nylon with a yellow cotton lining and a white fluffy padding in-between – just like a sleeping bag, actually! A resemblance heightened by all

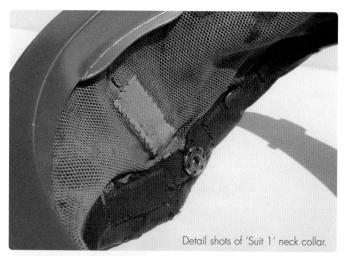

Detail shots of 'Suit 1' neck collar.

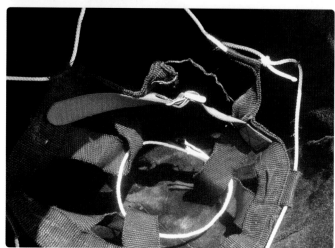

This shot and above: helmet straps.

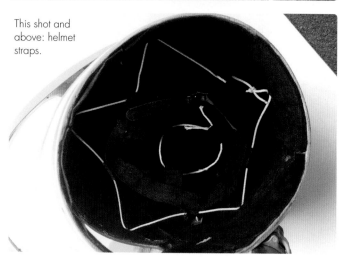

the large white zips (brand name *YKK*), most of which are sewn shut. The only add-ons, apart from the arm badges, are two fibreglass wrist arm/glove joints and two aluminium bands at the ankles, all four of which are just glued in place and could easily be removed prior to washing the suit.

The first (hand) wash removed a great deal of dirt but was complicated by the fact that the material acted like a giant sponge and absorbed nearly all of the water I was trying to wash it in, then threatened to fall apart under its massively increased weight. Luckily it dried rather quickly and I was able to sew it all back together again and patch a small tear in the back. Then I could safely wash it again – and again – and again! It really was that filthy, and in between washes I even resorted to using paint

Helmet undergoing restoration.

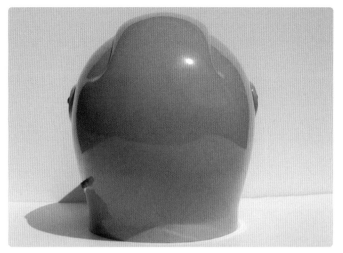

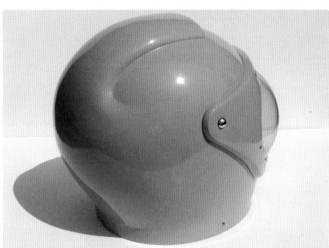

Badge detail on cleaned suit.

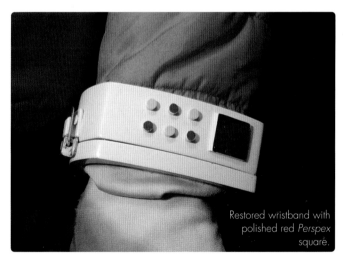

Restored wristband with polished red *Perspex* square.

thinners to try and remove some stains as well as having to scrub the interior to try and remove all the car filler that had been used to assemble the mannequin. Finally I let the suit dry and it was almost unrecognisable from its former state, the material which was decades old and slightly worn in a few areas now looked bright and new.

I could now reattach the two one-inch wide aluminium ankle bands, which had only needed a quick rub over with metal polish to restore them. I did actually put them on the wrong way round to begin with, by thinking that it made sense to hide the join on the inside of the leg. But the joint is actually placed on the outside of the leg so I had to switch them around with a mental note to myself to stop 'thinking' and just copy what had been done before. Unfortunately the two wrist connectors on the arms of the suit are rather heavy fibreglass castings that have a tendency to swing around when you are moving and clunk against any object you come across, meaning that they had been repainted many times to hide damage as well as having pieces of black tape applied to decorate them. It was a fairly simple task to sand all this paint off and fill any holes and cracks. The six buttons were missing and so I had to make those and then clean the paint off the red square, which is just a piece of coloured *Perspex*, and give it a polish.

The most damaged parts on the suit were the fibreglass glove connections. The gloves themselves are standard store-bought items, with a maker's label that reads *Les Leston*. They are rather

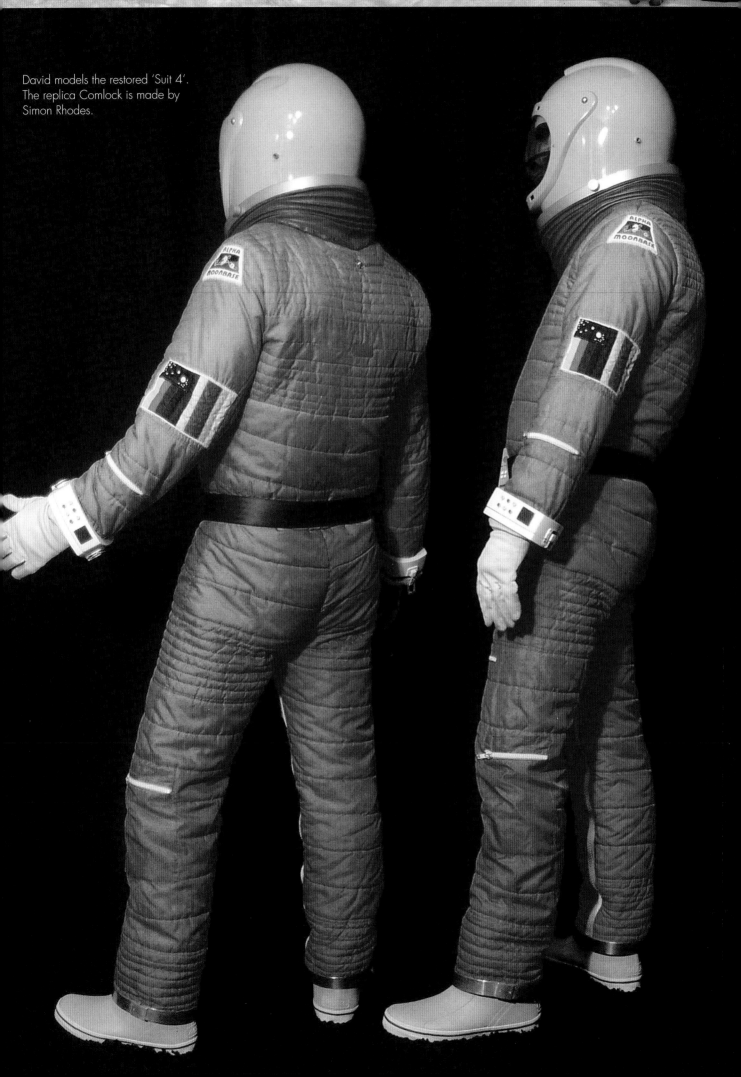

David models the restored 'Suit 4'.
The replica Comlock is made by
Simon Rhodes.

Before and after shots of the original Backpack.

comfortable and made from a silky white material with black leather palms. Unfortunately they are sealed onto the suit using a thin fibreglass ring that mates to the heavy wrist connectors, and both of these had shattered over the years.

Back in 1973 when the suit had first been made the gloves were simply joined to the suit using magnets, four of which are fixed into the heavy fibreglass wrist castings with matching metal plates buried in the glove ring. However, when filming began the magnets proved to be inadequate and simply couldn't do the job, and those who watch the show closely will often spot the gloves coming off during the various 'action scenes', especially when the actors started to have wrestling matches on the lunar surface! The first option was to apply clear adhesive tape around the whole wrist unit (meaning that the actor would not be able to remove the gloves without an assistant's help) and the final option was to fix very obvious metal buckles to the sides to lock the parts together.

The modifications to fit these buckles had involved drilling the thin areas of the castings, which had severely weakened them, and over the following years both glove rings had broken up – but luckily the parts were still glued to the gloves. So I carefully removed these parts, cleaned them, and then re-assembled all the fragments using superglue. These rough parts were matched up to the wrist connectors to make sure they were the correct shape and then all the gaps could be filled with *P38* car filler and sanded smooth. The gloves also needed multiple washes before being glued back onto these repaired pieces.

Sadly the helmet was almost as bad as the gloves had been: very battered and cracked, with a terrible paint finish and more bits of black tape stuck everywhere. Also the clear visor was missing, the visor frame was hanging off, and all the original screws and bolts were missing. The rubber neck piece was in a poor state and the spring-loaded parts that secure the helmet to the neck ring were also gone and had

been replaced by rusty screws that had been crudely forced through both the ring and the sides of the helmet.

The first job was to remove all the rotten cloth and the head support strapping from inside the helmet and then sand off the many layers of paint from the outside. The visor frame had the most layers of paint on – nine in fact – and had obviously come from a different helmet as one of the colours was silver – indicating its use on a second season Anti-Radiation suit. The biggest problem was the large amount of hairline cracks around the chin area caused by the helmet being quite thinly cast and flexing. As these cracks would quickly reappear after painting the only option was to add a new layer of fibreglass to the inside of the helmet to strengthen the shell and stop the movement. This has made the helmet heavier but it has done the job and stabilised the surface.

The visor frame also had a fair number of cracks but here I could only remove any loose bits of surface material and refill the holes. After the repairs were complete the parts were spray-painted with cellulose car paints and then rubbed down with a cutting agent to get a very polished finish. New pieces of black cloth were cut out, using the old pieces as templates, and glued into place, then the head straps were reinserted.

In most helmets foam padding is used to support the helmet on the wearer's head, but these helmets use a loop of strapping attached to the inside using metal loops buried in the fibreglass. This strap can be quickly adjusted to suit different sized heads and makes the helmet cooler to wear because the head isn't encased in foam – but it doesn't feel very secure.

Replacing the amber tinted visor proved to be a bit of a problem, as I could not find a shop that sold a selection of old fashioned bubble-shaped visors. In the end I searched several second-hand shops looking for cheap old helmets and managed to find a visor that did fit, but it wasn't perfect. Several years later when *eBay* appeared I could do a better search and found a supplier in America who sold new old-stock items, with one visor being a really good match. The new item is made from a very soft plastic, so it was easy to trim it to fit the opening, and then secure it in place using the six small screws that are visible on the outside. The small black rectangular openings around the visor frame are just holes in the fibreglass casting to let air in for the suit's occupant, and are simply covered across the back using a strip of black cloth. The visor was then reattached to the helmet using two screws with chrome dome covers (mirror hanging screws from a DIY store). The black 'intake' on the top of the helmet is only an illusion created using black adhesive tape, but it does have a row of air holes drilled across it. Many of these details were covered over in the second series of **Space: 1999** when the helmets got a fresh coat of yellow paint, and this helmet came without any evidence of the vertical vents on the rear which again were just black tapes. I do prefer the look of those vents so I will add them at some point in future.

The metal-looking neck ring is, in fact, just another fibreglass casting, and I had to repair several holes before it was repainted. The two spring-loaded neck bolts were made using epoxy filler blocks with brass rods embedded down the centre. The rubber neckpiece had been supporting the weight of the helmet for years and was compressed and deformed. I had to gently stretch it out and then apply more latex rubber to the inside to hold it in the correct shape. The outside was cleaned, and any holes patched with drops of latex before it was given a coating of watered-down acrylic paint. I am surprised that a rubber prop from the 1970s is still in one piece and hasn't turned to dust by now!

When I acquired the suit part of the 'deal' was for me to restore a damaged backpack and recreate the chest pack for a public display that was fast approaching. The backpack had the number 3 on it but it was actually the number 7 'stunt' pack used in the last few shows featuring 'punch-ups' on the moon's surface. As a result it was very battered and I had to strip the parts off it and apply more fibreglass to the inside to fill the holes and strengthen it up. The backpack and chest pack were originally covered in a fine mesh cloth, but only some rough bits were left on the backpack and they didn't look that original and were probably fake. The unit was covered in new cloth and the various detailed parts reattached. One of the four oxygen outlets was missing and I had to find a replacement, and they turned out to be simple motorcar brake pipe connections; the air-tube itself was coaxial television cable with the outer plastic removed.

During this time my intention was to construct copies for my own suit, but after working on these parts I realised that I didn't really like them enough to bother! The design and construction is rather crude and I actually preferred the backpack that *Koenig* wore in *Brian the Brain*, which I thought was far better looking – however, since that time I have seen the episode again on DVD and Blu-ray and now realise that it is even cruder and may just be a large plastic tray for putting dishes and cutlery on!

Since restoring the suit I have often looked for the original yellow boots to complete it, but they have long been discontinued. However, there are often similar looking boots for sale and the ones I have now are a pretty good match. I can't take credit for finding these as they were actually spotted by a person on an Internet forum, resulting in several spacesuit owners quickly buying a pair. The big difference is that the original boot was tied at the top meaning that it would conform to the actor's leg. These new boots are thicker rubber and hold their shape all the time, meaning it's hard to get them inside the leg and then they can be seen moving under the material! So I just cut off the tops to make them more like ankle boots and they work just fine.

I made the belt from car seat belt strapping with a *Velcro* fastening. The replica *Comlock* is made by Simon Rhodes.

The suit is reasonably comfortable to wear but it gets warm rather quickly, especially with the helmet on. Over the years I have watched actors wearing spacesuits in films and wished I was doing their job, but having worn a suit for a short length of time I'm really not sure that it would be that much fun to be filmed in it!

David's superb model making can be seen at:
www.davidsissonmodels.co.uk/

Interior of Backpack prop.

Hollow backpack

Meet The Collector

Come with Modelling:1999 on a guided tour of the amazing collection of Space:1999 garage kit 'ideas man' and dedicated promoter of the series, Todd Morton

Modelling: 1999: Todd, tell us where and how collecting Space: 1999 models and props began with you...

Todd Morton: I've built models since I was a young boy. I started out with **Star Trek** because it was already in syndication as I was around 10 years old in 1976. So I had built the *Enterprise* – although not a very good job of it – but it hung from my ceiling in my bedroom. I had an older neighbour who was into all sorts of things including sci-fi and building the models. He had built the *Eagle Transporter* and

had it hanging from a shelf in his room. I happened to see it hanging there and I couldn't stop looking at it. He let me hold it and I instantly was infatuated with the design and look of the *Eagle*! Being 10 years old I didn't know the meaning of waiting and, after bugging him for days on end to see it and hold it, he eventually caved in and gave it to me. There started the endless building of *Eagle* kits.

M: 1999: How did collecting 1999 then expand... how did you get in touch with other Space: 1999 modellers?

Todd: Collecting **1999** came way later in life... building the 12" *Eagle* every time it was re-popped, I'd grab three or four kits and build them over the years until I saw the *Product Enterprise Eagles* on *eBay*. I purchased them all and really that began my collecting from there! I happened on a forum – the *Eagle Transporter Forum* – and joined immediately. From there it seems like yesterday I only had a few *Eagles*. I met a few of the members who were very helpful and steered me in the direction of some great garage kit makers of some fabulous **Space: 1999** kits. I started gathering more and more kits and, along the way, was introduced to more kit makers and builders. My collection was

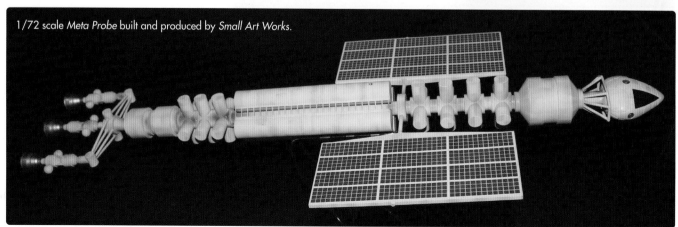

1/72 scale *Meta Probe* built and produced by *Small Art Works.*

1/72 scale *Kaldorian Sleeper Ship* built by Tim Nolan, produced by *Small Art Works*.

1/72 scale launch pad produced by Alex Dumas (*Sci-High Models*) and built by Jim Small.

1/72 scale *Deluxe Eagle* with lab pod and spine booster by *Round 2* built by Jim Small.

growing at a fast pace. I would be chatting with members and they would mention other members who were selling or making kits – most of which were in the UK or Canada. The people I met along the way really have helped me grow my collection and that is why I try to help others so much... it's kind of a pay it forward thing.

M: 1999: Tell us a little about your collection... What types of models and collectables does it include?

Todd: My collection is mainly the 1/72 scale models. These are the most available of the various scales and are/were all we had for many years – like the MPC 12" *Eagles* besides the custom built stuff. I do have a few 1/24 scale models, which is the same scale as the original 44" *Eagles*, and 1/48 scale now with the new 22" *Eagle* kits from *Round 2 Models*. I have over 25 *Eagles* from built up kits to the diecast *PE Eagles*, and some still in their original boxes. Each *Eagle* has something it brings to the table. There are six various *Eagles* with differing pods : *transporter*, *rescue*, *laboratory*, *winch* and *cargo* pods and I have all of them. There are also various attachments for the *Eagles*: *spine booster*, *side boosters*, *grab arm*, *glider* and, for the *winch pod*, also canisters marked Radiation. I also have the nuclear mines from the episode *Collision Course*. The launchpad is in scale with the 12" *Eagles*. I have all 3 *Laser Tanks*... a few *Moon Buggies*... So much to list!

M: 1999: Do you have any original models, props, costumes, etc. in your collection?

Part of Todd's collection.

1/72 *PE Eagle* winch with a magnet inserted in the grabber by Tim Nolan to pick up radioactive canisters, with *PE Cargo Eagle* in the background.

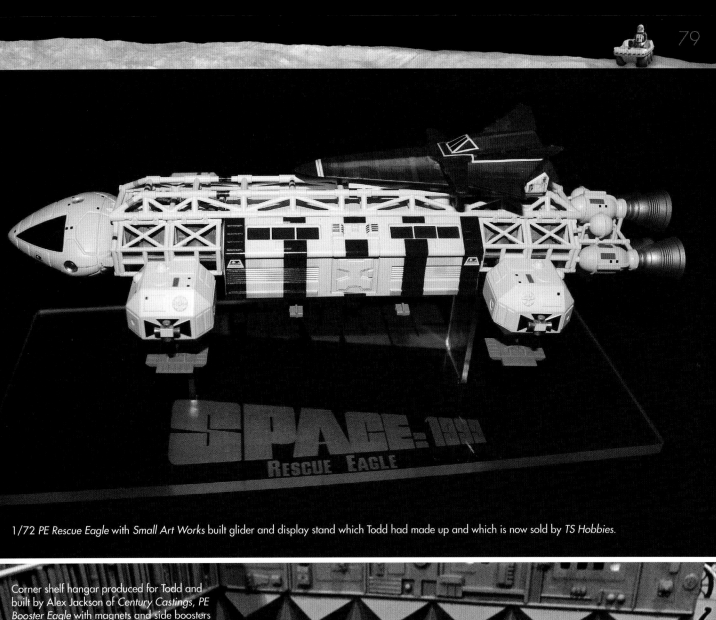

1/72 *PE Rescue Eagle* with *Small Art Works* built glider and display stand which Todd had made up and which is now sold by *TS Hobbies*.

Corner shelf hangar produced for Todd and built by Alex Jackson of *Century Castings, PE Booster Eagle* with magnets and side boosters built and added by Tim Nolan and *Collision Course* mine produced/built by JD Bryson.

Todd holding a scratchbuilt *MK IV Hawk* built for a model contest by Gary McMaster from the UK.

1/48 scale *Bueto Hawk* produced/built by Alfred Wong.

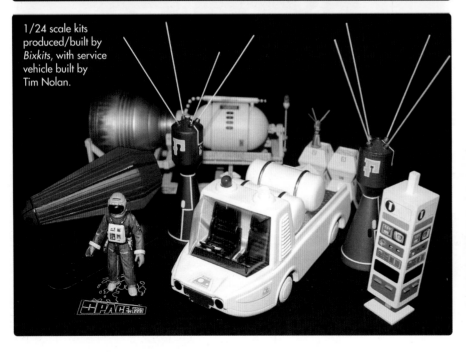

1/24 scale kits produced/built by *Bixkits*, with service vehicle built by Tim Nolan.

Todd: I wish I did have an original model from the TV show – it is my hope to own one someday!

M: 1999: What would you say are your top five pieces, and why?

Todd: My top five models... Let's see... that will be a tough one to answer.

1. My launch pad would have to be my favourite and most sought after model, along with the *Deluxe Laboratory Eagle* with *spine booster*.
2. The *Ultra Probe* is a favourite and very hard to come by. It's rare to see it in someone's collection.
3. The *Meta Probe* is also pretty rare and a favourite of mine.
4. I was very excited to find the *Kaldorian* sleeper ship – another rarity kit.
5. My *Swift* model is in the top five ships of my **Space: 1999** models – it's most intriguing if I may say so.

M: 1999: You are also involved in displaying items from your collection at shows. Tell us more about that.

Todd: I haven't done any shows just yet – my 22" *Eagle* will be on display at *WonderFest* this year, so that is exciting for me. We are working on a **Space: 1999** convention for 2017 and if that happens I will be displaying a huge part of my collection along with my friend Gordon Moriguchi and his 44" *Rogue Industries Eagle* and *Hawk* with accessories.

M: 1999: And you also produce, in conjunction with model makers, some very desirable and accurate replica props and models. How did this come about and what have you co-created for the 1999 collecting community to date?

Todd: I have worked with a few of the kit makers – basically helping advertise their

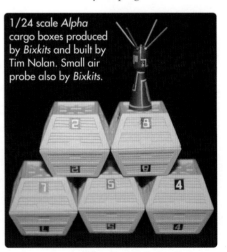

1/24 scale *Alpha* cargo boxes produced by *Bixkits* and built by Tim Nolan. Small air probe also by *Bixkits*.

1/24 engine and hoist produced/built by *Bixkits*.

1/72 *PE Eagle* with attachment for the JD Bryson mine with grabber and display stand by *TS Hobbies*.

much sold out already. Working with these guys is great for everyone who loves **Space: 1999**.

M: 1999: What can we expect in future from you?

Todd: We are working on a few things right now which I can't really talk about at the moment, but there is a 22" *Eagle* display kit in the works and hopefully a *Konami*-scaled corner shelf display hangar. In the *Facebook* group I post events 'Kit Alerts' to keep members up to speed as to what we are working on. I have a great imagination so I can dream up some really cool stuff.

M: 1999: What do you hope to add to the collection in future…What would be your holy grail 1999 item?

Todd: My next addition to my collection would be the 1/48 *Laser Tanks* and *Moon Buggy*. The holy grail would have to be a 44" *Eagle* and an original prop from the TV show.

M: 1999: How much of your life does this take up… and how much space in your home does your collection cover?

Well, since I started the *Space: 1999 Props & Ships Group* on *Facebook* it's taking up quite a bit of my time, which is OK with me because I really like the group and how it has become so popular and extremely busy. Trying to keep it fresh and updated is a tall order, for sure. As for my collection it is in my basement (the man cave) and it's starting to take over. I will update it later this year with some new display cabinets to show off my collection.

M: 1999: How can fellow collectors contact you?

Todd: Anyone wanting to contact me can use *Facebook* or email me at: toddmorton766@gmail.com

Photographs by Lori Miller.

creations but one producer in particular I do work closely with – basically throwing ideas at him – is *Century Castings* owner Alex Jackson. We just kind of clicked and became good friends and we bounce ideas off of each other almost daily. I tell him *hey, this would be a nice kit what are your thoughts and can it be done?* Alex has been casting props and other sci-fi related items for a while now. I asked him about a small-sized hangar for my 12" *Eagles* and we came up with the corner shelf

display hangar. It was a very nice kit and has sold well. He also did a group kit which included a *Stun Gun*, *Comlock* and *Comlock Holder* for the *Space: 1999 Props & Ships Facebook* group that I created and run. We decided to make a limited run of 100 kits and sold out. That was such a fantastic feeling and then to watch them build and finish them was special. I've worked with a great gentleman – BP Taylor – who has re-popped his *Eagle 1B* kit and it's pretty

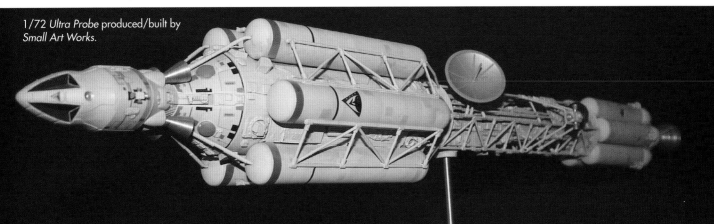

1/72 *Ultra Probe* produced/built by *Small Art Works*.

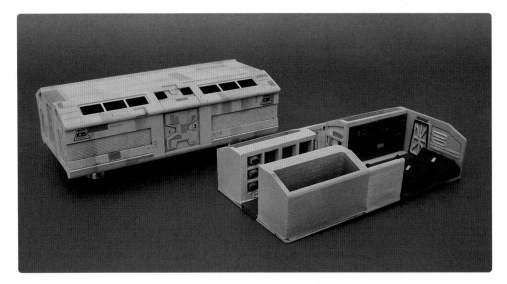

Passenger Pod
—the inside story
John Reason lifts the lid on the new 22-inch interior kit.

A late addition to the contents line-up for this publication was an example of a new resin *Passenger Pod* interior kit for the *MPC* 22-inch *Eagle* from *It's An Ashton*. It should be noted that the kit featured in this review is a prototype only, and, as a result, is of a less defined finish than the production kits will be, reflecting its 3D origins in the ridged texture of its walls and details.

Fast-approaching deadlines left little time to assemble, paint and modify the prototype if it was to be included in this title, although I *would* be able to shoehorn some small alterations and additions in within the timescale.

The kit comprises of a main floor with computer wall (integral in the review example, but upgraded to a separate piece – making it easier to access and paint – in the production kit) to which are added two storage units and a separate end door section. [Photos 1-3]

Each piece was first sanded then treated to several sprays of filler-primer, sanding between coats. The parts were then sprayed with *Tamiya Racing White* acrylic, an ivory-white I felt matched screen footage of the *Pod's* interior. [Photo 4]

The grey of the floor section was masked off and sprayed with a standard grey automotive primer. [Photo 5]

The computer wall was masked and picked out in grey, then adhesive paper labels, sprayed in the same grey, were cut up and applied to smooth out the wall's surface. Decals from the spares box were then used to suggest instrumentation, and the divisions between panels picked out with a permanent fine line pen.

Adhesive paper labels were also applied to the airlock door, having first pressed masking tape into the depression to determine the contours, the resulting

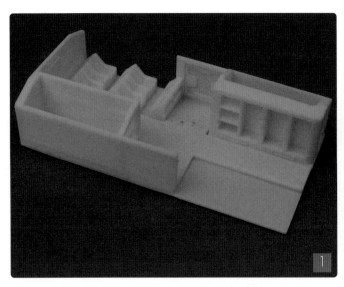

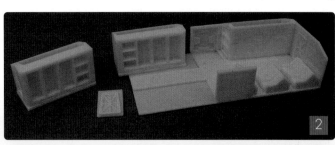

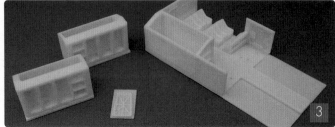

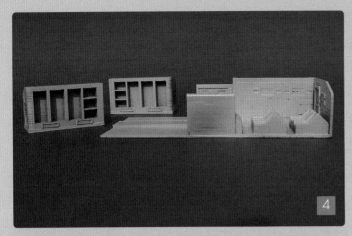

4

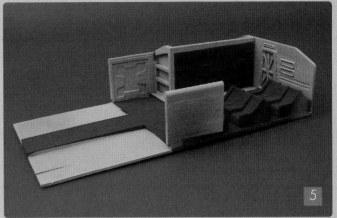

5

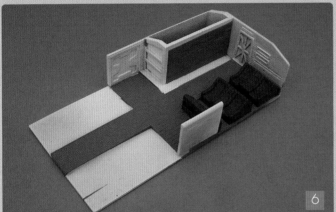

6

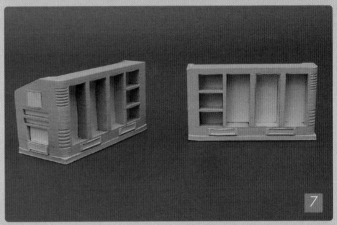

7

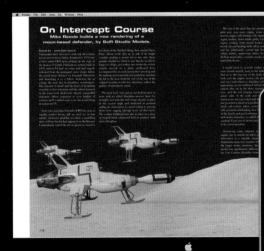

8

9

shape subsequently being cut out and stuck to the back of a label, enabling the door's edges to be followed. The door frame was also smoothed by supergluing pieces of white business card over the existing frame. The revised door and frame were then brush painted in white acrylic.

Seating was brush painted in matt brown [Photo 6] and, again, decals were used to suggest instrumentation, with small squares of paper label being stuck into the depressions between the seats.

The storage units seen in the live action set (plus the side wall of the computer section) feature a number of 'light box' illuminated panels on their fronts and sides. These were reproduced by inserting pieces of white business card into the depressions then painting the framing edges in matt white. [Photo 7]

I decided to create three spacesuits and helmets to occupy the alcoves in one of the storage units (as they had on the live action set). I cut simple spacesuit shapes out of white card, then primed and painted them, drawing on details in pencil, shading them and finally coating them with satin acrylic varnish. Small squares of balsa were stuck behind the suits to lift them from the rear face of their alcoves and make them appear to be suspended when glued in position. The helmets were created from metal beads from a discarded necklace my wife gave me for the spares box, these being primed then sprayed signal yellow. The visors were then

brush-painted on in clear orange and framed with a fine line pen. [Photo 8]

After being superglued into the storage unit the helmets were shaded on their bottom edges with *Europe Earth* weathering powder then sealed with satin acrylic varnish.

The various white grills on the storage units and walls were picked out in matt white with a brush. Had I had sufficient time, I would have sanded off certain of these that featured misshapen borders and added scratchbuilt replacements.

Cut down kit parts and 'shapes' from the spares box were added to the side wall of the computer section to represent various pieces of equipment.

Finally, the two storage sections were superglued to the floor and the kit was complete. [Photos 9-10] Unfortunately I didn't have a spare unmade 22-inch *MPC Eagle Passenger Pod* to assemble around the interior, but have shown the kit here

next to my completed pod to demonstrate how snugly the piece will fit into its dimensions. [See opening shot]

10

Conclusions

An ambitious, unusual and welcome addition to the **1999** kit universe. Some work was needed to improve the finish, although I am assured by the producers that the production kits will be smoother than the example these offices received. Even so, bearing in mind the current limitations of 3D printing some careful sanding, filing and filling will be needed and should be expected. As the storage units and computer wall are hollow pieces, opportunities are presented for the ambitious modeller to backlight these sections should they wish to do so. One can also imagine cut-away *Pods* being modelled to display separately from the actual *Eagle*, and also *Pods* with opening doors to reveal the interior. The possibilities are many and exciting and we look forward to seeing them...

The *It's An Ashton Pod Interior* kit is priced at £70 GBP, including worldwide delivery, and full details are available via an email to: itsanashton1999info@gmail.com

Exclusive!

COMING SOON: Brian Johnson's new designs and models will feature exclusively in
Sci-fi & fantasy modeller.

Exclusive!

Now there's a **Modelling: 1999** section in *every issue* of
Sci-fi & fantasy modeller.
Read about the latest **1999** kit releases, plus step-by-step builds and *Sixteen12* 44" Eagle updates.
Subscribe NOW to avoid disappointment at: **www.scififantasymodeller.co.uk**

Alpha tanks 0, Infernal Machine 3

Olivier Cabourdin builds surface defence for the wayward Moonbase

This article chronicles the building of more additions to my **Space: 1999** kit collection in the form of the three *Alpha tanks* which appeared in the episode *The Infernal Machine*, in which they were destroyed rather quickly! Despite their very limited screen time, the tanks have become objects of desire for many **Space: 1999** modellers.

They also featured very briefly in two other episodes: in the teaser at the beginning of *The Last Enemy* and in the *Eagle* hangar in *Space Warp*. Although they seem similar at first glance, there were three different models built, but with identical weaponry consisting of a laser cannon.

While nothing was said in the show to explain the sudden presence of these tanks in *Alpha*'s inventory, the common

explanation is that they were converted construction vehicles used to build the *Moonbase*, with original crane, shovel or rockbreaking equipment having been replaced by powerful lasers.

The SFX models were motorised, as their chassis were based on 1/25th scale *Tamiya Chieftain Tank* model kits which featured electric motors to drive the tracks, and were built by Martin Bower in just few days.

The resin kits featured here were produced by James Small, and are in scale with *Product Enterprise*, *Airfix* and *Warp Eagles*. They each require a supplementary donor kit – the 1/72 *Airfix Chieftain Tank* – to provide axles, wheels and tracks. The tanks are each identified by a letter in the instructions. I don't know

if this is canon, but at least it is useful.

Model E is the most recognised of the three as it has a cockpit inspired by the *Eagle*'s beak. From my point of view, this is the coolest of the variants. The studio model had an entry hatch at the rear that was a part taken from the **2001: A Space Odyssey** *Aurora Moonbus* model kit. It later lost this part when Martin Bower recycled it as part of a new model for Gerry Anderson's **Into Infinity**.

The *Model H*, or 'dome laser tank', has a viewable driver in a bubble dome. It seems to be inspired by *Tintin*'s lunar tank in *Explorers of the Moon*. *Product Enterprise* produced this model in a set also including their 11" *Eagle* with *laboratory pod* and *boosters* and a small *Moon Buggy*.

Model F, also known as the 'flat top laser tank', has a camera and spotlight at the front of the vehicle. The driver sits in a larger bubble dome than that of *Model H*.

The scale of the resin kits is usually given as 1/72, in line with *Product Enterprise*, *Warp* and *Airfix*. As for the latter, the scale is an endless debate that navigates between 1/72, HO and 1/100. In other dioramas I have included 1/100 *Alpha Moonbase* characters from *ERTL* kits, and they scale very well next to *PE Eagles*.

So... how accurate are these kits when compared to the original models? Overall, they're pretty good. A few shortcuts have been taken with details, but these seem to work. Curiously, *Model E* (with the *Eagle*-like nosecone) shows some raised panels that would normally only be created with decals or paint. I decided to keep them, but on the topside of *Model F*, near the bubble cockpit, I removed some pipe detailing that shouldn't be there.

The quality of the moulding is average... there were lots of air bubbles and a lot of cleaning work to do, plus flash and warping to deal with. On the other hand, the white resin was easy to work with.

Assembly began with the wheels, tracks and chassis. Each wheel is in two parts (the inner side from the *Airfix* kit and its resin counterpart outer) and, since there are eight wheels on each side of each tank, this comes to ninety-six parts for the wheels alone! Although they were not included in the kit and not mentioned in the instructions, I also had to add further tiny wheels (three per side, so eighteen more wheels to dig out of the *Airfix* kits). These were used to hold the upper side of the tracks on the *Chieftain Tank*. Cleaning of the parts was tedious, and needless to say all this occupied me for several evenings...

On the resin sprockets (toothed wheels) most teeth did not survive the casting process. I therefore made new ones using *Airfix* parts, removing the central dome from the resin parts with a punch and saving these. Some of the resin tensioning wheels (small, toothless ones) were oval, so I had to repeat the operation, again using parts from the *Airfix* kits, to remake them. On the chassis, many of the axles had not survived the casting process and as the remaining one inspired me with little confidence as it would surely not had supported the track tension, I cut away and replaced all of them with metal rods.

There were some bubbles on most parts on each of the models, and the problem was that their number increased approximately threefold because of further underlying examples, appearing after the first cleaning and sanding work had been carried out. I therefore applied my 'hedgehog' method: filling the holes with plastic rods and superglue. This is much faster and efficient than using putty.

Some wedges were needed to align the box rows on the back shelf of *Model F*. The front part of the model was slightly bent,

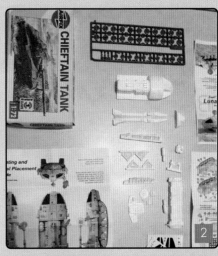

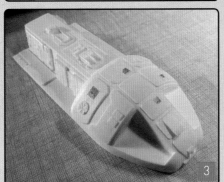

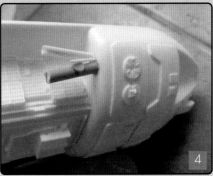

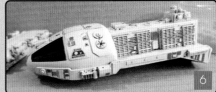

Model E

1 & 2: *Model E* has a cockpit inspired by the *Eagle* beak. I personally think this is the coolest of the three tanks. A 1/72 *Airfix Chieftain Tank* is needed for the wheels and tracks.

3: Inaccurate panels highlighted in pink, that I finally decided to keep.

4: Bubbles were filled with plastic rods superglued into the hole, cut and sanded to shape.

5: *Model E* with off-white base colour.

6 & 7 (see overleaf): Left and back side of the *Model E* body, painted, decals and black wash applied, and awaiting the matt coat.

this being corrected following a quick bath in hot water. The gun barrel of the model was wrong and needed to be sanded to the correct shape. While cutting the vacformed cockpit dome, I realised I was unlucky and found a fold I had not seen when first opening the box. Not having the time to make a new master when I built these models, I used it as is, glued with repositionable *Microscale* glue so I could easily remove and change it later.

At the rear of *Model H* there was a large bubble in the 'drum' part that it was better to replace completely. The detail was redone using tree parts from a plastic kit, the cladding being created simply with *Tamiya* tape. Some grooved parts are very thin on the guns, and I had 'fun' cleaning

then and redoing some using spare flash material lying around on the workbench.

Like other **Space: 1999** Earth vehicles and ships, the base colour is not pure white, but slightly off, so I mixed *Tamiya Matt White* with a few drops of *Sky Gray* (*Tamiya XF-19*). Placed against white, the mixture looks grey, but in a darker environment the eye and camera accommodate it as a white.

The provided decals were of average quality: some had an apparent printing frame, and the colours were too dark (the orange was more of a brown-red, for example). I therefore ended up airbrushing on most of the grey, black and orange panels. After a coat of clear varnish, a light black wash was applied to

7

Small Art Works
Lunar Tank
Model "F"

Excellence In Model Building

www.smallartworks.ca

8

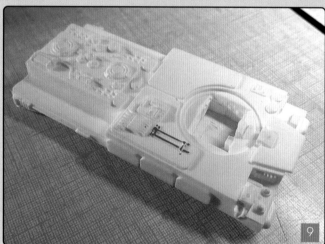

9

10

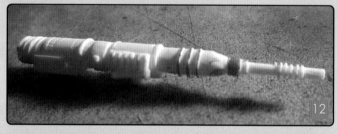

12

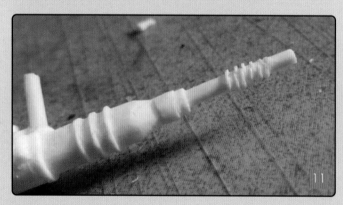

11

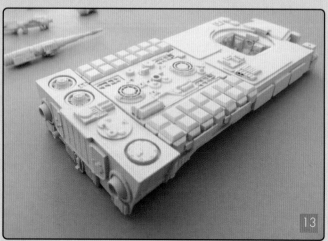

13

14

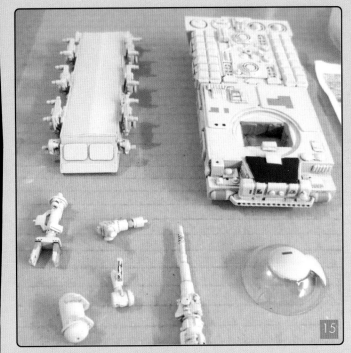

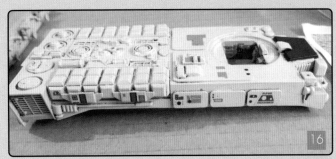

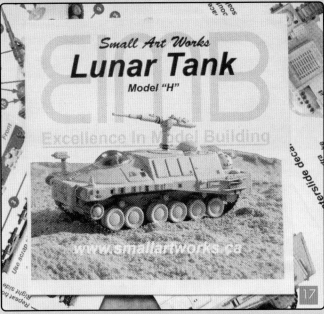

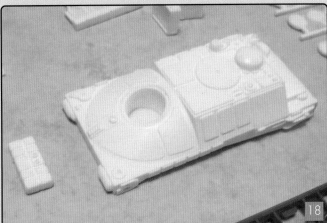

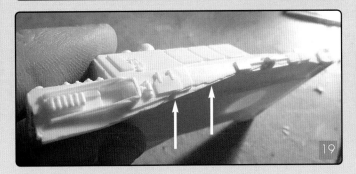

Model F

8: *Model F* is the flat top lunar tank with the large cockpit dome. 9: On the topside, near the bubble cockpit, some pipe details were superfluous and were removed. 10: Some wedges were needed to align the box rows on the back shelf of *Model F*. 11: Due to the casting, some parts of the thin raised rims at the tip of the gun were redone with resin spare flash material laying on the workbench. 12: The gun barrel of *Model F* is wrong. All the details highlighted in pink and the 'bottle' neck need to be sanded to the correct shape. 13: *Model F* with off-white base colour. 14: The cockpit dome had a fold I had not seen when opening the box. 15 & 16: *Model F* painted, decals and black wash applied.

highlight the details, followed by a matt clear coat (*Prince August Air*) thinned with *Tamiya* thinner (this trick avoids white marks).

Final assembly brought a trouble spot in gluing the soft plastic tracks, on which none of my glues seemed to work. After surfing on military model websites, it seemed that there was no miracle solution! The tracks were bent to the correct shape by heating them near a candle flame, then glued directly to the wheels with rubber-enriched gel superglue which adhered here a little better than classic superglue.

As the models are small, I decided to build a base to highlight them on, and, once again, I chose a lunar surface, as I had done for my other **Space: 1999** dioramas. To create this I took some foam board (here a failed part from a first try at

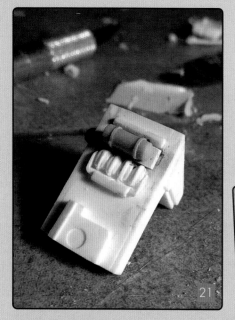

22

24

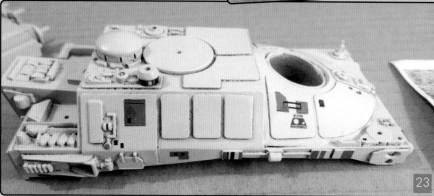

23

Model H

17 & 18: *Model H,* or 'dome laser tank' – this seems inspired by the *Tintin lunar tank.*

19 & 20: Moulding gap and bubbles.

21: There was such a large bubble in the 'drum' on the rear section that it was better to completely replace it. It was redone with some tree parts from a plastic kit – the cladding was simply made using *Tamiya* tape.

22: *Model H* with off-white base colour.

23: The main body with all the painted panels, decals and black wash applied.

24: Parts of *Model H* ready for the matt clear coat.

25 & 26: Comparison of the model kit and its *Product Enterprise* cousin (with transparent 'cable').

Wheels and axles

27: The provided toothed wheels were replaced by their counterparts from the *Airfix* kit, retaining the tiny central dome from the resin part.

28: 'Doctor, I need a tablet!' Once punched from the resin wheels, the little domes were sanded to level them and glued to the *Airfix* parts.

29: Resin axles were replaced by metal rods.

30: The diorama used at conventions to exhibit the tanks is a lunar surface completed by a background composed of *NASA* photographs of the Moon and starfield.

25

my launch pad diorama) with a half-arc shape completed with the rise of a lunar dune. The ground was shaped with a heat gun, and covered with a mixture of black oil-based paint and roughcast. Then a light grey was airbrushed on, keeping the flow in the same direction to result in a very dusty effect. The background is an image from scanned *NASA* photos of the lunar surface, with a large starfield added at the back, printed on poster photo paper. As this was 70cm long, I had this produced via a printshop on the net.

26

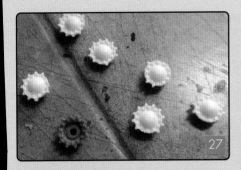

The Forgotten Eagle

Robert S. LePine creates a unique Space:1999 diorama

Looking back at how this adventure started I have to make a confession up front. I knew that everyone would be going bananas doing up their *Round 2* 22-inch *Eagles* to a high degree of finish, as accurately as they could, and as quickly as they could... I, however, kind of walk a different path. For example, I finished an old *MPC Eagle* years ago in a 'lunar

camouflage' paint scheme that I thought really worked. [Photo 1 and 1A]

So, and armed with the new *Round 2* kit, I started my plan for a new Lunar Camo.

It failed. [Photo 2]

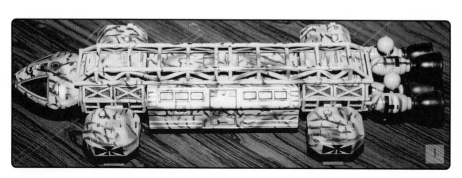

I needed a new direction, so I began looking on the net for an idea that might work – lunar images from the moon landings, that type of thing – and then it hit me: some of the Geometric Camo schemes that are used on modern combat aircraft. An *F-18* in wargame colours gave me a further direction.... and thus the second paint job began on the *Eagle* and, after many hours of masking and painting, masking and painting (Did I mention, masking and painting?) this was the result—see Photo 3.

I *hated* it!

So here I was with a model I had waited most of my life for, and I had failed twice in finishing it to my satisfaction. What do you do with a model of this calibre after giving it this many coats of paint? Stripping something like this would be a major undertaking and it would never really be the same ...but you can't walk away. So, what you do is you go on social media – *Facebook*, to be exact – and you find a friend. Todd Morton and the *Space: 1999 Props and Ships Fan Page* to be exact. You

1A

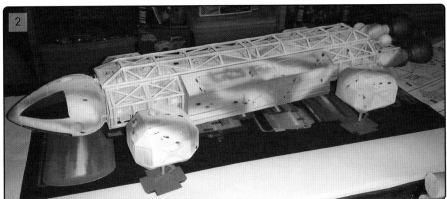

2

3

and the current Space Program has been suspended until further notice. All *Eagle* production has been halted. It seems that the blame for all of the Earth's woes has been placed squarely on the shoulders of the men and women who were involved in the removal of all of the nuclear waste from the planet – an action that subsequently caused the explosion that removed the moon from the Earth's pull. A few engineers, scientists and one brave pilot have stolen away the last production *Eagle* right off the assembly line and hidden it for future generations...

This, alas, is not to be. Eighty years later she still waits... *Forgotten.*

I want to make it known that this model diorama was a mistake right from day one. Nothing went according go plan. However, positive comments, inspiration, and the fact that this kit was very important to me made me determine that I would never give up... this diorama being the eventual result of that approach.

OK. That was the introduction. This is the nitty gritty. You all know what the kit's like so I won't cover that here...

As a pattern maker I have access to good tools, materials, and to ways of making almost anything I need for my job, my home and my hobby. This does give me an advantage on occasion.

The base of the diorama is 3/4 plywood, with hardwood trim around the outside, sanded, sealed and painted. The floor of the scene is a combination of *Lexan* and particle board to give the illusion of concrete I wanted to create. However, I also wanted a *Lexan* base so that I could effectively glue the building to it... hence all the layers. The building structure is all 1cm cut *Lexan*, which is extremely strong and flexible, and is great to work with using any type of good solvent cement. I did my best to try and keep the structure as close to 1/48 scale as I could (years ago I had watched and assisted in putting up a

post your *screw up*, and an individual comments (I wish I had this gent's name so I could give him credit) about how much this paint job reminds him of how the *Eagle* looks like it has just come off the production line and hasn't made it to the paint shop yet and B I N G O – I have a plan!

Imagine this: the opening sequence for a new motion picture. It has been months

since the moon was torn out of Earth's orbit on September 13, 1999. The destruction and devastation caused by the changing gravitational fields has left many parts of the planet in ruin

building like this). The walls are all sheet styrene, the barrels are *Tamiya* 1/48 accessories, and the little dog came from an *ICM* 1/48 scale *German Luftwaffe Ground Personnel Set* given to me by my buddy Greg.

The overall paint scheme was shades of grey. I'm not going to say *fifty* – it might have been closer to *thirty* (LOL). The kit was built straight out of the box with no modifications, no lights, nothing – a *what you see is what you get* approach. The display was built up using basic architectural techniques – if you use a square and a small level you can't go wrong. If you have access to an industrial plastic supply operation then *Weld On #3* is very useful, and is what I use for all my model assembly work. This stuff is great on styrene, *Lexan* and most plastics. I have to warn you, however, that it will destroy *old Airfix* plastic (pre mid-'70s).

Weathering the *Eagle* and the scene was a process of trying everything from enamel black wash in the tight areas to acrylic washes overall, then using glass cleaner and *Q-Tips* to clean up the staining effect. ...And Pastels. *Mighty* pastels! That's the secret! Use black, rust and brown and scrape these into powder form. Then, using any brush of choice, rub the powder onto the model wherever you feel it will look good. Stand back – and if you don't like the result in any area glass cleaner will remove it and you can try again. *Dullcoat* through your airbrush will then seal the pastels onto the model. For heavier staining with pastels rub them onto the model directly from the stick, streaking down in the direction of gravity with your fingers, or a *Q-Tip* or a brush. Remember, this is a trial and error process – just go for it and have fun!

The scenery was a combination of toy plants (from the dollar store), railway ground scenics, celluclay, enamel and acrylic paints – plus twigs and branches from the back yard, applied, of course, with carpenter's glue and CA glue (thin and thick versions).

I worked on this project off and on for over six months to create a take on the *Eagle* that I feel is unique and unusual. I hope I've inspired you as now it's over to you to create your own 'not seen on screen' scene featuring this classic ship.

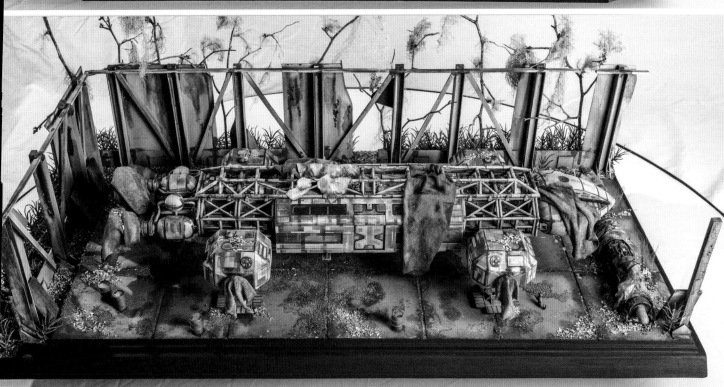

Space:1999 Studio Scale Masterpiece Collection
—exclusive update

We hand over the following spread to Steve Walker of *Sixteen12 Collectables* for the latest news on the production of his upcoming studio scale 44-inch Eagle replicas...

Steve: Well, I'm delighted to be able to officially announce the launch of our **Space: 1999** *Studio Scale Masterpiece Collection*, which will not only feature *Eagle 1* at 44-inch scale, but also a 44-inch *Laboratory Eagle*, a 44-inch *Rescue Eagle*, a 44-inch *Cargo Eagle* and a 44-inch *VIP Eagle*. Edition sizes will be strictly limited to 200 worldwide for *Eagle 1*, 100 worldwide for the *Laboratory*, *Rescue* and *Cargo Eagles*, and just 20 copies worldwide for the *Limited Edition VIP Eagle*.

We are really excited to have this opportunity to come back to the **Space: 1999** licence, as a 44-inch studio scale *Eagle* was always something we had wanted to explore when we were producing our die-cast range of spacecraft and, of course, our 23-inch *Eagle* replicas.

We have assembled a team of *Eagle* experts to advise and ensure accuracy, and have also gained access to some very comprehensive reference materials. Further, we are utilising cutting edge manufacturing technologies to ensure that our models will be the most accurate 44-inch studio scale *Eagle* replicas ever produced.

We fully appreciate that collectors are eager for news concerning the development of the editions, and therefore thought it would be a neat idea to chronicle the progress of the models in the form of a detailed online 'diary'. This will focus on every aspect of the construction and tooling of the *Collection* plus the evolution of packaging design and decal artwork through to actual production of the finished models themselves. The diary can be found on our website and will be updated regularly as work progresses.

Finally, I am able to reveal that our licence includes the reproduction of a 31-inch *MK IX Hawk* studio scale replica. We are exceptionally pleased to have the opportunity to tackle this beast (my personal favourite guest craft from the series) and, as I write this, production is already well underway on the tooling model. We are sure this will be an extremely popular subject with **Space: 1999** collectors and, with an edition size of

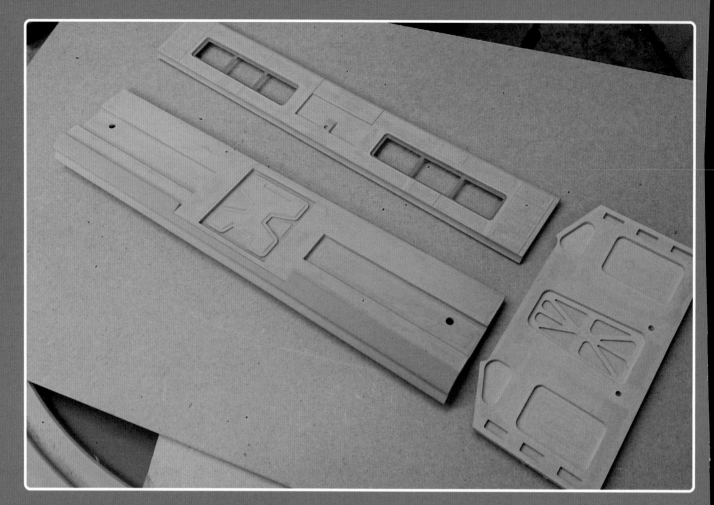

just 100 models wordwide, the *Hawk* should prove to be a highly desirable replica and investment.

More information on the *Masterpiece Collection* can be found at our website: www.sixteen12.com

Editor's note: In addition to Steve's online diary, regular updates on progress of the Space: 1999 Studio Scale Masterpiece Collection *plus exclusive photographs and insights will feature in each Volume of:* Sci-fi & fantasy modeller.

www.scififantasymodeller.co.uk Subscribe today!

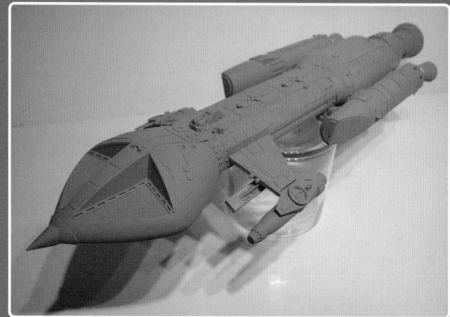

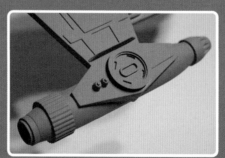

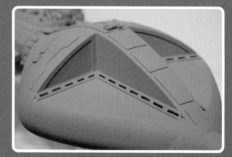